EASY
KEEPER

EASY KEEPER

. . .

Mary Tannen

Farrar   Straus   Giroux

NEW   YORK

Library of Congress Cataloging-in-Publication Data
Tannen, Mary.
Easy keeper / Mary Tannen. — 1st. ed.
p. cm.
I. Title.
PS3570.A54E2 1992 813'.54—dc20 91-35917

Chapters 5 and 7 originally appeared in
The New Yorker

For Maria and Bob

EASY
KEEPER

CHAPTER 1

■ ■ ■

Conners Creek

In 1886 Jared Conner, with his partner, an unknown Frenchman, came into the region hunting elk for the hides and antlers alone. Settlers, who relied on elk for food, were outraged when they discovered Conner's kills rotting on the ground. A delegation rode out to Conner's camp, about three miles east of the present town of Priest Creek, to demand a stop to the slaughter, only to be met by the wrong end of Conner's shotgun and some harsh words. The settlers returned that night and lynched both men from a cottonwood tree beside the creek that today bears Conner's name.

—from the Priest Creek *Crier*

LILY WAKES, as she always does, at five. The dream she was having evaporates, leaving a salt trace of anxiety, a feeling that something must be done. She sits up in bed and listens, but hears only the usual sounds, the rooster's crowing, the peacock's unearthly cry, the soft pat-pat of her brown poodle half-breed, Gravy, heading downstairs. Lily's bedroom is in the original part of the house. Some time ago, Lily and her husband, Jerry, added a sitting room on the other side with a bedroom above it. Jerry has that room to himself now. Downstairs, Lily checks to see if he has passed out in his chair or on the floor. The room is empty. She adds wood to the stove. She puts on overalls, parka, hat, boots, and gloves.

Bright orange Mars is rising with a crescent moon. The wind is in the south, bringing warmer air. It will be clear and sunny for the sheep shoot, as Dusty is calling it. The shoot might explain Lily's sense of—what? Emergency, something she must do right away, an urgent matter that has slipped just beyond the edge of consciousness. She reviews the plans in her mind: Dusty is bringing George Strick, the photographer; the Turrells, Chris and Irene, are trucking in a couple of merino sheep and a Herdwick ram. It will be a full day and, as always when animals are being transported, a day with plenty of opportunities for the unexpected, mishaps, accidents. But it's the kind of day Lily enjoys. She's done her preparation and feels up to it. Expect the unexpected, that's her method. She shakes herself, as an animal might. It's a trick she uses to get rid of something that is weighing her down.

Jake, the Manx ram, comes to the fence and regards her with a solemn expression that belies the absurdity of his four horns, two sticking out like party hats at rakish angles, two curled under at the sides like a pageboy hairdo. He's her court jester, her wise fool from one of Shakespeare's tragedies. She feels there's a message in his eyes.

His head turns to follow her on her rounds. First to the chicken coop, because the turkeys will pester until they're fed. She puts out grain for them and for the chickens, places eggs in a wire basket. Then to the barn, warmed by space heaters, fragrant with the mixed scents of hay, milk, and the dry, herbaceous droppings of sheep. This is the maternity ward, where ewes and nursing lambs are kept. Through the night, Lily keeps a light burning and a radio playing easy-listening music to comfort the lambs in their first weeks of life.

Twin Manx lambs come bobbing on stiff legs to nudge and butt against her. The bums, she calls them, because they suck from beer bottles since their mother refuses to nurse. Lily milks the cashmere goat and empties the pail into bottles labeled Moosehead and Pacifico. The lambs crowd their woolly backs between her legs as she sits on a stool, holding the bottles. An old song of Jerry's comes on in an elevator-music arrangement. It used to turn her over inside every time he sang it. She never would have thought it could be made into this bouncy tune, but if you take away the words and Jerry's voice, it has a nice melody. The lambs' tails switch with the beat.

The Turrells are right on time. Lily lifts their son, Ian, down from the truck. When the sheep have been unloaded and settled in pens, Lily invites the Turrells in for coffee while they wait for Dusty. She puts Ian in a high seat she keeps for her friends' children and gives him cookies in the shape of dinosaurs.

"Where's Jerry? Is he dead?" Ian asks, more gnome than child in the ski hat he refuses to take off.

"He's sleeping, honey." Irene reaches across to wipe her son's face.

"I think he's dead." Ian looks over his shoulder at the stairs leading to Jerry's room. Ian's afraid of Jerry. Most children are, although Jerry, if he notices them, is friendly. He used to say he wanted kids of his own, but Lily wouldn't. She told him his chromosomes were too screwed up. His DNA must look like spaghetti. They'd have mutants, babies with no arms. It's been a long time since he's talked about having children.

Chris and Irene are staring into middle distance, sipping coffee. They have curly hair that falls forward and small amber eyes. Lily imagines that under Chris's beard he has a long upper lip and receding chin, like Irene. "The trouble is that they look like sheep and their ranch lacks curb appeal," Dusty said when Lily suggested that his story "Wool Gatherers of Priest Creek" should be about the Turrells exclusively. Although Lily shears her sheep and sells the wool, it's not the main enterprise of her ranch. The Turrells raise sheep primarily for wool; they spin it into yarn, weave it into cloth. But their ranch looks utilitarian, with prefab barns and a modular house. Dusty has always wanted to photograph Lily's ranch, which he says has style. When he proposed his story to *Western Life* magazine, he showed snapshots of Lily and her place. The Turrells don't mind. They think the American public should know more about sheep and are happy to truck their livestock to Lily's more picturesque surroundings.

Dusty's already an hour late when he turns into the winding dirt drive that leads to Lily's house, but he stops on the bridge over Conners Creek to let George admire how the broad cottonwood trees lean out across the water. Dusty tells the story of how the creek got its name, something he just finished writing up for the Priest Creek *Crier*.

"Then they named the creek after the man they lynched," George says when Dusty has finished.

Dusty shrugs. "Maybe they felt guilty, or maybe the name just attached itself to the creek and was made official after people had forgotten the reason. See that big old tree with the spreading branches? Get a shot of it, why don't you?"

George rolls down the window and takes a picture. "You mean that's the hanging tree?"

Dusty shifts into low to get up the hill. "I was thinking of putting it in the piece, but Lily probably won't let me. She says that hanging tree would be long gone by now. The cottonwood grows fast and dies young." He's quiet for the rest of the way; he wants George to see for himself how Lily's unpainted wooden house and barns fit into the land, how the mountains rise all around.

"Nice," George says. Dusty nods.

They pull up in front. Dusty puts his hand on George's arm. "Just one thing, sometimes her old man gets coked out and loses it. He ran me off the place with a .22 once. It's all right—I mean, Lily hides the shells now—but I wouldn't want you to get taken by surprise or anything."

"Maybe I'll stay in the truck."

Dusty laughs. "No, he's harmless. Scary-looking, but too wasted to do damage."

Lily hears them in the mudroom, taking off their boots. "Lily believes in preventing dirt, not cleaning it up, so if you bring in mud, it'll still be here when you come the next time," Dusty is saying. She opens the door.

"Lily, this is George. He's come all the way from Denver to take portraits of sheep. Damn funny way to make a living, if you ask me."

"Hi, George." Lily shakes his hand. "God, Dusty, that hat." It's Day-Glo green and has *Priest Creek* stitched across the front.

Dusty grins. "Like it? They gave it to me up at the Howling Coyote in appreciation and partial payment for judging the Jell-O Jump contest." The Turrells stare at Dusty's hat, but they don't comment. Lily pours coffee.

"Where's your old man, sleeping?" Dusty points his beard toward the ceiling.

"I'd better look in on him—" she says.

Dusty grabs her wrist. "Let sleeping dogs lie, know what I mean?"

Of all Lily's friends who come and go, there's only one whom Jerry doesn't like, and that's Dusty. Dusty has never liked Jerry either. It's one of those natural antagonisms. You see it all the time in animals. Humans generally hide those emotions, but they are present anyway. Jerry has messed up his mind so much that antipathy has degenerated into paranoia. The time Jerry fell down the stairs and cut his head, Dusty helped take him to the medical center. Jerry was ranting on about how Dusty had pushed him, even though Dusty had been in the barn with Lily when it happened.

Lily listens at the bottom of the stairs and hears nothing. It's not unusual for Jerry to sleep through until evening. It would be nice to have him quiet and out of the way until the shoot is over.

They set up pictures of merinos, their coats being sheared off in wide ribbons, of Ian feeding the bums, of mouflons escaping over a fence. Dusty has George take one of Chris cheek-to-cheek with the Herdwick ram. It's a little cruel, because they look so much alike, but maybe Chris doesn't mind.

Around one o'clock, Lily goes to heat the soup she made yesterday and slice the bread Dusty brought. Jerry isn't in his chair. She takes out some beers, and lemonade for the Turrells, who don't drink alcohol. They eat sitting on fresh bales of hay that Dusty has stacked by the barn for effect. The sun is strong. It must be sixty degrees. Melting icicles drip from the eaves with an urgent, broken beat. Inside the barn, a man is singing on the radio to someone who saved his life. "Let me stay awhile," he sings. "Let me stay forever for a while."

"That's Jerry's song," Chris says. "Ian, Jerry wrote that song. That's him on the radio right now."

Ian jumps up, about to say something or ask a question. Irene pulls him toward her. "Have another cookie," she says.

Jerry wrote that song sitting on Lily's deck, to thank her for letting him stay and get strong and healthy putting a new roof on the barn, and building a bridge over Conners Creek. It's the song the band played at their wedding. The royalties paid for the new addition on the house. It's the song that put Jerry back on tour. When he returned, he said he wasn't doing hard stuff anymore, just pot once in a while—it helped him relax—and a beer now and again, nothing wrong in that, was there? But she noticed he couldn't meet her eyes.

She gave him work to do. He made the kitchen cabinets. Weeks went by. She thought the ranch and the work had cured him again. Then he met someone by chance on Main Street, someone from Los Angeles whom he'd known on tour, who sold him some cocaine. Jerry said it wasn't addictive. Lily said it didn't belong on her ranch and ordered Jerry to get rid of it or leave.

Lily wasn't afraid to live alone. She'd grown up an only child in a large house, with parents who were preoccupied with unnamed problems of their own. She'd always pictured herself living with only her animals and therefore had had no doubts in sending Jerry away. It was after he'd left that she learned about loneliness, guilt, remorse, and second thoughts. Then the call came from Denver: Jerry had nearly died in a hotel room there. She went to see him in the hospital (against Dusty's advice) and brought him home. Jerry would be all right for a time, and then someone would come to town with cocaine or pills and get in touch with him, and Jerry would disappear. The first few times, Lily was frantic, then she got used to it. He'd always come back, subdued, ready to get into his projects around the ranch, although the music stopped completely. Then he began doing drugs at home, which Lily rationalized as being better than going off somewhere among strangers. The times when he took drugs began coming closer together and there was drinking when he couldn't get drugs.

Lily started sleeping on the other side of the house. The adjustments were gradual. It's only when Lily hears a song from the old days that she realizes what's been lost.

"That's the second time today I've heard that song," she says.

Ian has to use the bathroom. Dusty's in the one downstairs, so Lily takes Ian up to Jerry's. While Ian is in there, Lily opens the door to Jerry's room. The air pushes against her face, damp, feral, like the breath of a large beast that has been shut inside, hiding in the night that Jerry makes out of day, with his blackout curtains, his dark sheets. Ian comes and leans against her leg.

"He's sleeping," she says, and turns the child to get him out. He ducks past and runs to Jerry's bed. She steps over clothes, beer cans, soda cans, and pulls Ian away, not looking at Jerry.

"He's dead," Ian says.

"This is a good little stove." Dusty is stoking the fire.

"It's a winner, isn't it?" Lily says. "Throws off all kinds of heat, and that wood, it's the same wood I put in this morning—"

Dusty turns sharply, afraid, or hoping, she'll break down. She's been too calm. Dusty took her to Petrillo's for dinner and she ate as if it had been days since her last meal. Now she wishes the Turrells hadn't thoughtfully taken care of the chores. She'd like to go out to the barn and work through the night.

Animals die on the ranch, of accidents or natural causes. She doesn't like finding them dead, but she has developed procedures. When she saw Jerry, she didn't know what to do. She pulled Ian out of the room and shouted to Dusty to call the rescue squad. Dusty came up the stairs, quick and light for a big man. He took Jerry's wrist, then dropped it and stepped away, rubbing his own hand against the side of his corduroys. "Lily, I think we'd better call Rick. There's nothing we can do now. I'll call Rick and let him know," he said. Rick, because he's the sheriff. Buzzy came too. It confused her at first, seeing Buzzy, because he's her tennis partner; they play in the doubles tournament together. Then she remembered that he's also the coroner.

Dusty is working another log into the stove. "Why don't you open that bottle of red wine I bought?" he asks. "It's on the kitchen counter."

She's trying to figure out why Dusty looks different. It's his hat—he isn't wearing one. He always wears a hat, summer and winter, indoors and out. He must have removed that terrible hat in deference. He's gone nearly bald. From the back, crouched by the stove, he could be twenty years older. Dusty twenty years older. Jerry dead. All since this morning. And still the flames have been licking away at the same pieces of wood. There's no such thing as the march of time. Time isn't an army on the move; it's unrelated bits. Some stand where they are and some jerk forward. The only way they don't go is backward.

Jerry had a mop of hair that fell across his forehead like a boy's, still growing even today while they were taking pictures of sheep and running in and out of the house, while Jerry's song was playing twice on the radio. The body doesn't die all at once.

The heart, Buzzy said, stopped early in the morning, when Jerry inhaled some cocaine, and the brain stopped seconds afterward. The blood gradually trickled down through the large and small channels of veins and arteries. That's why his face was gray and the back of his neck, when Buzzy lifted the head, had dark purplish streaks. The neck and jaw were stiff. Buzzy said that rigor mortis was setting in, which probably meant Jerry had been dead a long time. "How long?" Lily asked. "I could calculate it —there's a formula—if I knew the temperature of the room. The higher the temperature, the faster it happens," Buzzy said. "This is a cold room," Dusty said. "Lily's concerned that she could have saved him if she'd come the moment she woke up." Buzzy looked from Dusty to Lily. "I'm pretty sure he died before then," he said.

Dusty is watching her from the kitchen. "What's that, St. Vitus' dance?" he asks.

"Regrets, shaking off regrets."

Dusty finds two glasses and motions for her to join him on the sofa.

When Lily was twenty, she went home from college for her father's funeral. Her mother was in a black wool dress, sheer black stockings. Her fleshless feet in narrow black pumps clicked across the floor as she went from telephone to door to telephone, arranging everything.

"I don't want to speak ill of the dead," Dusty says.

"Don't."

"You know what he was, Lily."

She holds a hand up to stop him, and to block the sight of his face, so filled with blood, every corpuscle swollen with it, the hairless top of his head shining from the race of platelets. She can feel the wool of her sweater itching at the point where her blood pumps through the jugular vein, her lungs greedily taking in air. She understands why she was so appalled by her mother's energy, because it was fed by the joy of being alive, the relief of not being a thing, an object that people discuss and dispose of as quickly as possible.

The sheriff and the coroner, broad Rick and slender Buzzy, were standing beside the bed. "No sense causing Lily trouble over this. I'm going to put down massive heart failure. That all right with you?" Buzzy sounds as if he's speaking through rain. Where other voices speed, his slows and becomes more distinct. She'd wondered at it before, but seeing him in his capacity as coroner, she understood.

There aren't many old people in Priest Creek. As a result, most of the deaths Buzzy encounters happen like this one, in the middle of life, when no one is looking for it. Buzzy's developed a method for getting past the event that leaves most people catatonic, stupefied, unable to think of what comes next. Buzzy is the one who appears and begins to reassert order. He writes down the probable cause of death. He knows the procedure for disposing of the object that is no longer a person. Bill Pease does have a hearse, but it seemed an unnecessary expense to call it. And it probably couldn't have made it up the hill. So they wrapped Jerry in his dark sheet; Dusty and Rick carried him out and laid him in the back of Dusty's pickup. Dusty said he was light.

He's taking it lightly, sitting in Jerry's house, drinking wine, talking about calling people they know to give them the news. He helped Lily decide to have Jerry cremated and scatter his ashes by the creek. Jerry had never said what to do. He never expected to die. He must be so surprised.

"There were accidents," Dusty says. "The time he passed out with his head against the stove. You saved his life plenty of times."

"Not today, and I knew it, or I knew something when I woke up. If I had gone to him then—"

"Hey, don't get into that." Dusty puts his arm around her shoulders. "Don't think that you knew then what you know now. It's a trick the mind can play. There wasn't a chance you could know that today was different from all the other days he's slept through until night. He was a walking phantom. He gave up life a long time ago. It's not your fault."

It's not Dusty's fault either, he wants to tell her, even though his heart is rejoicing that it has happened at last. He was here once when Jerry vomited in his sleep. Dusty watched Lily clean it up, so calmly and matter-of-factly that he knew that she must have done it, and worse, many times before. He found himself wishing that Jerry had choked and drowned on it. You read about people doing that, why not Jerry?

They wound him tightly in his sheet, and Dusty helped Rick carry him out. A corpse is supposed to be heavy, but Dusty didn't notice. Of course, he was carrying the legs; Rick had the shoulders. They let him down in the back of the truck, and even Buzzy, who's used to being around the dead, raised his eyebrows when the legs hit the metal.

Dusty holds Lily close. He rubs her back, her arms, but she's stiff with grief, or guilt more likely. He has to save her before remorse coagulates into rigor mortis of the soul. He pulls the afghan around her shoulders and begins searching through the bookshelves. He gave her a copy of the I Ching once—where is it, does she know? When he gave it to her, he said it was the book of changes, that she could find answers in it. She replied that most of her questions could be answered by a veterinarian.

He finds it on the top shelf and blows off the dust. Does she have the coins he gave her? She must have them, she says, but can't think where they are. No matter—he'll make do with a quarter. Toss it, he tells her, and she does, while he marks down one dash for heads, two for tails. Are you sure this is the way it's done, she asks. It's the way I do it, he says, pleased with himself for having distracted her, for having thought to call on the Oriental wise men, masters of changes. He marks her throws, the long lines, the broken ones, each beneath the other, until he has the six-level house. He settles his reading glasses on his nose, flips to the index of hexagrams, finds the one that matches hers, and turns to the text.

"What does it say? You have to tell me." She thinks it must be something damning, words that will scar her, a punishment.

"Bites on old dried meat and strikes on something poisonous. Slight humiliation. No blame." He gives her a significant look over his glasses.

She laughs for the first time since it happened. "It never makes sense to me. I think you have to be a thousand years old and Chinese to understand it." Still, she grasps at the last sentence, "No blame."

CHAPTER 2

Brownian Movement

DUSTY SCRAPES the warm sticky batter onto the floured board. At first flaccid, it gathers strength under his kneading until it acquires the elasticity and density of living flesh. He gathers it up and slams it on the board. Flour rises, swirling into space. "Cosmic dust at the dawn of creation!" he shouts, loud nonsense to cover troubled thoughts. But he only wakes Lorraine, a brindle boxer, who rises and stretches in the cosmic dust, now transformed by sunlight into a shower of gold. Oblivious to this splendor, she shakes herself, sending particles into a frenzy, and thrusts her muzzle between Dusty's legs. He opens the back door and follows her out, both of them stepping, without having to look, around the holes. He should replace the entire deck, but lumber's expensive.

The thaw that began the day Jerry died continues. There's a faintly vegetal odor from primitive plants that live on the margin of climatic disaster—rock-clinging algae, lichens, mosses—coming out of dormancy, venturing a cell division or two in the warming sun. It could all close down tomorrow under a foot of new snow, but these primordial survivors know just how far to trust the thaw. They don't overextend, don't expose too much.

Lorraine follows her dog trail through the snow to the creek. The water gets a thermal boost from hot springs upstream. Even when it's frozen over, there will be occasional breaks in the ice and wisps of vapor rising out. On this mild day, a layer of mist hovers over the creek like a spirit reluctant to leave its body.

Yesterday was the ceremony for Jerry. All those jeeps and trucks churned the drive up to Lily's into a river of mud. Dusty's thinking of going over today and laying some logs in the really bad spots.

Although it was warm in the sun, the snow was still hip-high by the creek. Lily had told everyone to bring cross-country skis. Dusty's been to a couple of weddings on skis but this was his first skiing funeral. He thought it gave the procession a festive air. The guests were quiet, respectful —not a sound when they reached the creek besides the clicking of water over stones and the rasp of a ski or two. There was even weeping—some of the women and Chris Turrell, who stood with tears streaming into his beard, like a ram in the rain. They couldn't have been crying for Jerry, who hadn't a friend there (his family wouldn't come). The tears must have been for Lily.

When Dusty first knew Lily, she was a glamorous figure, for Priest Creek anyway. She was young and had her own ranch, while other people her age were still messing around waiting tables or assisting carpenters. True, she'd bought the land with her inheritance, but she was serious about it; she worked hard. Dusty was interested—then again he was interested in most attractive young women, still is— but she wasn't someone you could meet in a bar and take home for the night. Her land, her sense of purpose, demanded more. In the back of his mind, Dusty had a feeling that Lily Dusquesne was someone he'd like to know better, in a couple of years, when he'd established himself, when he had something to balance what she had.

Then Jerry came like a sick animal to her door and she took him in. What did he have to offer but his unappeasable need?

Yesterday Dusty held the brass box. A cardboard one

would have done as well, but the undertaker had insisted on brass and Lily hadn't the will to argue. Dusty opened it and offered it to Lily, who reached in with bare hands. The ashes were flaky, gray, like what you'd find in the bottom of the fireplace. Dusty scrutinized bare branches of cottonwood trees as she let the ashes out over the snow. Why didn't she toss it all into the water?

Conners Creek runs into Priest Creek, which marks the edge of Dusty's spread, his half acre. When the real thaw comes in a month or two, Jerry's ashes will wash into the water and race by Dusty's door, tumbling over stones on a thundering course to the Pacific.

Over at the corral, Lorraine touches noses with the chestnut mares, Horse I and II. Dusty rents them to tourists in summer, one of his many ill-paying sidelines. There's a town ordinance against keeping horses, but Rick Starrett overlooks it in Dusty's case, since Dusty lives at the end of Paradise Road, which itself is across the creek from the rest of town. The road used to be outside the legal limits of the town, a convenient arrangement back then, because Paradise Road had been lined with brothels and bars, which were outlawed in Priest Creek proper. Those old places are gone, except for the Lost Dollar Saloon, which remains dedicated to its original purpose.

Since 1968 there's been a new social hub of Priest Creek. Once again it lies outside the town limits—Ski Town, three miles north. It is Marietta Boyle, chief stockholder of the corporation that owns and operates Ski Town, who is keeping Dusty home when he would rather be helping Lily repair her road.

Marietta summoned Dusty a week ago Tuesday to lunch at Chez Marietta, her restaurant at the top of the gondola. Dusty went eagerly, as Marietta is the largest employer in town and Dusty has worked for her many times. He's taught skiing on her mountain, sung ballads in her restaurant, even conducted tours of prospective buyers through her condominiums. This time Marietta was calling on his expertise as self-appointed town historian. She was already at her table, sipping a Campari-and-soda. She gave him wine—a new Chardonnay she had just laid in—ordered a salad for herself and the salmon coulibiac for Dusty.

She began by giving him an overview of the ski industry, which was leveling off. There were no longer enough new skiers to keep it growing. Resorts were going to have to compete with each other for a limited number of skiers. Priest Creek was within easy driving distance of nowhere and, because of the altitude and changeable weather, often impossible to fly into. "I'm afraid Priest Creek is going to go under unless we find something that will make people choose it over the bigger, more accessible resorts," she said.

Dusty looked out at the brightly dressed skiers on the slope. He knew Marietta was not after more lift-ticket money. Even at thirty-some bucks a day, it wasn't enough to support the ski mountain. She wanted to attract people who would buy her land and build condominiums and second homes. He thought of everyone he knew who had come here to live: Lily, the Turrells, even Dixie and Shane, who shared a trailer behind the Safeway parking lot. "People come here because they have this fantasy about the West—"

"The myth. The myth of the Old West," she said, beaming like a teacher whose favorite student has just come up with the right answer. He'd made her happy. She poured him another glass of the very decent Chardonnay. "Priest Creek is an old Western town. It's just as authentic as any of them—like Telluride—and our snow is better," she said.

"Telluride has all those Victorian houses," Dusty reminded her. He didn't have to say how Priest Creek had squandered its heritage. Marietta knew as well as he did that Main Street, with its parking lots, gas stations, and

plate-glass and aluminum storefronts, could be found anywhere. It has no singularity. Every week in the Priest Creek
Crier Dusty runs a picture of one of the old buildings,
along with a piece that tells where it stood, what it was
used for, and some colorful story attached to it, if he can
find one.

"There's not much we can do with the town physically.
I'm badgering the Town Council to put up historical markers and fake gas lamps, but I thought if we could find a
story, some legend of the Old West that could get people
thinking of Priest Creek as a real Western town . . ." For
a person of such corporeal bulk as well as such material
wealth, Marietta is surprisingly cerebral—holds a degree
in philosophy from Bryn Mawr. She led him to a window
where they could see the town neatly laid out in the elbow
of the creek. "I know there's a story there," she said. Marietta has a weakness for melodrama.

"The trouble with the history of Priest Creek is that it's
one of false starts and broken dreams—not enough gold
or silver for mining, too far from the stockyards for cattle
ranching, too high in the mountains for farming. The only
success Priest Creek ever had was with skiing," Dusty told
her.

"Why does the legend have to be about money? Why
can't it be about love?"

"A Ute warrior and his bride—"

"No Utes," Marietta cut him off. "Indians are too sixties,
too love beads, leather headbands. Besides, the Utes didn't
leave written records. I want a verifiable love story, a legend
of the frontier. There must be one lying around in the
records. It's a matter of going through them with an eye
trained on love."

Dusty agrees with Marietta that the history of Priest
Creek must have its share of love stories, but finding one
will be difficult. Love isn't written on the public record and

leaves few physical traces. There isn't a Taj Mahal or Albert Monument in town. How do you leach a love story from the lists of marriages, births, and deaths, the tailings of newspaper articles?

Lorraine is back, her duties as resident dog accomplished for the day. He lets her in and turns to the table strewn with clippings, photos, gleanings from the cartons of materials that Ellie Stern, town librarian, let him take from the basement, or "archives," as she calls it.

Ellie was at Lily's yesterday—her good round face. The whole town turned out to comfort Lily in her sorrow at the loss of her love, although no one pretended to know why she'd loved him, or why she let him stay so long.

Everyone brought something to eat or drink. It's customary in Priest Creek when there's a death or other catastrophe for friends and neighbors to draw around with food, sympathy, whatever is required—kind of like white blood cells rushing to the wound. Many people in Priest Creek originally come from cities, from places where people lead more isolated lives, but once they spend a couple of seasons here, once they've turned their Cherokee over in a ditch or had a tree fall across their driveway, they learn the necessity of neighborliness.

After they came back from the creek, everyone was hungry and fell on the food. They were eating and drinking, catching up on local news, until most of them forgot why they were there. Dusty almost did. He'd look over at Lily every once in a while and she'd be talking sheep with the Turrells or getting a beer for someone. She was doing fine. She seemed to move through the rooms with a new lightness and ease. As their friends circled, talking, eating, laughing, they infused the house with their spirit. Their energy drew Dusty and Lily closer together until, as the last group left, Dusty was standing in the doorway with his arm around Lily and he felt her body soften into his.

Dusty is sorting his material according to year. Organization is the secret. Love is often presented as a chaotic force because it breaks down old systems, but love is the ordering of emotions around a central theme. Dusty has to put the material together in the correct way so the love story will emerge. He goes through the old photos of all those people long gone, staring unflinchingly at the camera: the Priest Creek baseball team, the members of the Elks Club, the nurses gathered on the steps of the hospital. Their stern wooden faces give no hint of love.

Lily turned her face toward Dusty and he could easily have kissed her. He has no trouble kissing women—far from it. Many times he's opened his eyes in the morning to see tangled hair on the pillow next to him and regretted yielding to the impulse to kiss an upturned face.

Marietta said she wanted a tragic love story, and Dusty said that was understood, as all love was tragic eventually, because sooner or later one of the two falls out of love, or dies, leaving the other bereft. When Dusty's mother died —Dusty was told that she went to heaven—Dusty's father quit his job, packed whatever he could in the car, and took off. No doubt he would have left Dusty behind too if there had been someone to take him in. They traveled, finding new towns, new jobs, new schools, sometimes twice in the same year. Dusty assumed his father was trying to find her again, while Dusty was certain that if they'd only stayed home she would have come back to them. (Dusty actually did go back to that first house, on a short street in a small town in upstate New York, after his father died. She wasn't there.)

Is that the reason why he didn't kiss Lily when she turned her face toward him? Is he afraid of love? Or was it she who turned away first? However it went, there was a change between them, and the next thing Dusty knew he was skiing to the creek behind Lily. They were wearing those lamps that strap around the head. The snow, crusted over since the afternoon, rattled under their skis. She stopped and they switched off their lights. The moon wasn't up yet, but the stars were bright. When their eyes became accustomed to the dark, they could see a smudge or a shadow lying across the snow.

"It wasn't a good idea, leaving him out like this. His soul can't rest if he isn't buried."

Soul was a word he'd never heard her use before.

He put his arm around her (an awkward maneuver on skis) and told her how different cultures disposed of their dead, beginning with the Indians of the Plains, who made platforms or tied their deceased onto trees so the birds could tear them to pieces and carry them to heaven, ending with the Egyptians, their methods of wrapping and preserving. He concluded by saying how all methods of disposing of the dead had two purposes: one, to safely remove the putrefying flesh so it would not contaminate the living; and two, to furnish the living with a means of parting with the dead. There was nothing they could do for Jerry's soul. The task was to get over him; to go beyond.

The dough, fat and soft, has swelled in the bowl. It sighs when Dusty buries his fist in it. He forms the loaves and tucks them into their pans. They look like doughy humunculi, limbless, blind, trusting. He covers them with a dish towel for the final rising.

When Dusty turned his headlamp on again, the ashes disappeared in the bright glare, as if they hadn't been there after all. The two of them were sweating when they reached the top of the hill, and thirsty. Dusty, at least, could have used a glass of wine. He unbuckled his skis and opened the door, but she put her body in the way. "Thanks, Dusty. I'm tired now. I think I'll go to bed." She touched his shoulder. "I'm sorry," she said. He had a devil of a time steering his pickup down her driveway with all that mud. It needs some logs laid over it.

The sun has reached its zenith and is now streaming through the skylight onto the papers spread across the table, making a ladder of light for dust motes to ascend. The dust is flour mostly, with pollen and spores that drifted in from outside, some debris from shooting stars—it comes right through the cracks in the walls—and some of Jerry's restless ashes that clung to Dusty's sleeve when Lily let them out of the box. Are they actually going up or only milling around, bumping into each other in the endless zigzag dance known as Brownian movement?

CHAPTER 3

Getting There without a Map

WHEN DIXIE MEETS someone for the first time, the story she likes to tell is how she drove all the way from Florida to Priest Creek without a map.

The first thing she did was remove the back seat from her Toyota and line the floor and sides with heavy plastic—tacked it in with a staple gun. She threw in some fresh straw for her goat, Betty May (named after her husband's girlfriend). René and Freddy, the rat snakes, rode in their aquarium on the passenger seat, and the shoe box with their babies in it on top of that. Floribunda, the pregnant hamster, stayed in her cage on the floor, and the black-and-white shepherd pup, Jewel, rode on Dixie's lap or down with Floribunda.

The way Dixie found Colorado was: she drove to Ohio and turned left.

The Colorado she was dreaming about was Denver—not Denver as it turned out to be, but Denver as in John Denver, that song of his that went, "Take Me Home, Country Roads . . ." which made Dixie think of a dirt road past a log cabin shaded by ponderosa pine, Betty May grazing in the yard, and a sweet, sad-eyed man playing guitar on the porch.

Or fiddle—violin—since the man she was going to see

played violin—Robbie. He was her high-school sweetheart. Nights, they used to lie out on his blanket and trace the constellations. Robbie went to college and she married Bruce. There must have been something she liked about Bruce, but she forgot it pretty quickly. He started messing around with Betty May (the girl, not the goat) and Dixie woke up one day realizing that her life had taken a wrong turn.

Driving to Colorado, with her animals in the car and her future a clear road ahead, she had never been happier, and maybe never will be again.

As it turned out, Robbie had an apartment, not a log cabin. It was in one of those singles complexes. There was no room for a goat, so Betty May stayed in the car. Robbie wasn't prepared for the animals, especially the snakes. After a few days Dixie could tell it wasn't working, so she kissed Robbie goodbye—no hard feelings—and drove on to the mountains.

She likes to say she stopped in Priest Creek because the stink of the sulfur springs covered the smell of Betty May, but what really made up Dixie's mind were the high meadows and dark fir forests. And the town didn't look fancy, like a lot of ski towns, more like the kind of place where someone like her could find a log cabin on a country road. She hasn't found it yet, however. The main problem is money. She makes only six dollars an hour at Louis's upholstery shop ("Our Work Stands Up When You Sit Down").

The baby snakes escaped from their box. Dixie had to give Betty May to a rancher. René and Freddy died. Floribunda ate her babies and then she died too. The only one left is Jewel.

CHAPTER 4

■ ■ ■

Disappointment Pass

Some say Disappointment Pass was named by Bibleback Burton, who homesteaded a ranch up there and would have starved if his brother hadn't rescued him. Others say it was named by prospectors who tried to but couldn't find gold. Then there are those who claim the pass just attracts disappointment to it. Take your choice.

—from the Priest Creek *Crier*

JEWEL RUNS HER TONGUE over Dixie's nose. Dixie lets her out and sees the sun coming up on the other side of the Safeway. The gumweed by the concrete block that serves as a doorstep is stiff with frost. Dixie shivers and closes the door. She gets back in bed and curls up against Shane, just for a minute, she tells herself.

Now the sun is oozing in bright and hot around the edges of the window shade. "What time is it?" She struggles against Shane's arm laid across her chest. What does she care, he growls. She promised Lily she'd be there at nine. He knows that. Dixie's been talking about it all week, bringing it up, hoping he'd come.

What's he going to do anyway on a weekend without her—drink beer and watch TV—when he could be riding up to the Continental Divide. He says, yeah, tending a bunch of hysterical New Yorkers, everyone on a horse from a different outfit. It's going to be a real rodeo and he doesn't want to get involved. She has to be crazy to go.

Lily asked her. Dixie was out in the Safeway parking lot, looking for Jewel, and Lily was walking back to her pickup with a bag of groceries. Dixie knows Lily to say hi to, but they hang out in different crowds. Dixie's mostly with Shane and the wranglers who work over at the Eden Glen Guest Ranch, and Lily's more tied in with the families of Priest Creek, the ones who own land. When Dixie waved and Lily stopped to talk, balancing her bag on her hip and shading her eyes with one hand, Dixie felt kind of flattered. They were talking about how their summers had gone and Lily mentioned the pack trip she was planning up to the Divide. She'd never ridden the trail off Disappointment Pass before. Dixie started telling her what it was like, how she and Shane rode up there all the time (really just twice, once this year and once last). Then Lily said why didn't Dixie come with them, that she could use someone who knew the trail and could handle horses, who knew how to pack a horse, something Lily had never done.

Dixie doesn't remember saying she actually *had* packed a horse before. Lily assumed it because Dixie was part of that group that works at Eden Glen. While she was talking to Lily, Dixie felt as if she could pack a horse—she'd watched Shane enough times. Then too, in the back of her mind she was thinking she could persuade Shane to go with them, so the moment would never arrive when she would find out if she really could pack a horse.

"I don't think they'll be hysterical. They're Lily's friends," Dixie says.

"Everyone from New York is hysterical—anyway, everyone who has the money to fly to Colorado for a weekend." He throws back the quilt. "You'll see," he calls over the waterfall of his morning piss. "They'll want you to take care of them and their horses. Just wait until they come up on one of those five-foot rattlers lying across the trail."

Shane's thinking of the kind of people who go on the Eden Glen trips, who pay a hundred dollars a day and expect the wranglers to do everything—pack horses, make the fire, cook, and wash dishes. It occurs to Dixie that Lily might have asked her because she was hoping Shane would come along. That makes her feel bad, because she hasn't been able to get Shane to come, and it would mean Lily didn't really want Dixie in the first place. She doesn't know if Lily would do that. She doesn't know Lily very well. Dixie likes the way Lily's place looks, sitting up above Conners Creek Road, and she admires the way Lily has made her life to suit herself instead of just letting it take her over, like most people Dixie knows, but Dixie has never actually sat down and talked to Lily.

Half-past nine already. Dixie pulls up the shades, even though Shane is still naked. If anyone's prowling the edges of the Safeway parking lot this time on a Saturday morning, they're welcome to look. Shane has a cowboy tan: just the bottom half of his face, his neck and forearms are brown. The rest—his forehead where the hat shades it, his chest, legs, and butt—is white as cream. He's working for the county now, chipping and sealing the roads. This winter he'll be doing overnight repairs at Ski Haus. Sometimes he gets a job taking out a horse pack trip for Eden Glen, where he'd like to get hired full time. Because Shane is really a cowboy at heart. You just have to look around his trailer to know that. The only things on the wall are two posters: Gary Cooper in *High Noon* and a scene from *Shane*. He keeps his saddle on a sawhorse by the door and his Stetson on a peg above it. He wears his Stetson, never a trucker's hat like the other men on the road crew.

Dixie hands him a mug of coffee. "So long as you're up, you think you could help me pack the horse?"

"Don't tell me *you're* going to be doing the packing."

"I've watched you plenty of times—"

"Yeah, but watching isn't doing."

"It's just what you do with the ropes on top, the double diamond hitch part, I'm not sure of. If I see you do it again, it'll be fresh in my mind."

"She's bringing you up there because she thinks you can pack a horse, doesn't she?" He pushes the pizza box from last night over to one side and sits on the table.

"She asked me because I'm a friend and she knows I'm good with horses. Besides, if I can cover a chair I can cover a horse."

"Chairs don't bite; they don't kick, and they don't go up and down mountains. Is there any beer left?"

Shane, steering with one hand, holding a Pacifico with the other, laughs when he sees them in the turnout at the head of the trail. She can't be serious, he says, meaning Lily. She has Dusty's two fat mares, renowned bitches who can't be separated. Lily has her own mule and Arabian, both young and green as sticks, and there's an Appaloosa that doesn't belong with either set.

"What took you so long?" Lily asks.

"Oh, this and that." Dixie jumps down from the truck, avoiding Lily's pale eyes, which spook her sometimes. Maybe tonight in the tent she'll tell Lily that Shane made her a deal: he'd pack the horse if she'd blow him while he sat on the table—with his boots on, his feet in the chair, his narrow white butt on the table next to the pizza carton. So she's late, but it's worth it, because Shane can pack a horse better than anyone. Then again, she might not tell

Lily. She isn't that easy to talk to, because she watches while you speak and then waits a second before she answers. It's as if everything mattered to Lily, even the words she looses into the air. Dixie just says things, and a lot of times she's surprised by what comes out. There must be a whole other brain operating in her voice box.

Lily's friends, Foster and Meg, do look like Eden Glen guests. Their hair is cut into styles like you see on TV, and they pat Dusty's mares with little tapping strokes on their noses. Dusty winks at Dixie and hands her a beer. He fusses around with the stirrups and saddles, giving Lily's friends a lot of advice about what to do if the horses—he's calling them Death Wish I and II—buck and rear, when he knows his mares can't even get two feet off the ground at one time.

Shane is packing the panniers and shaking his head over practically everything. He picks up a container of yogurt and looks at Dixie.

"This is the first pack trip I've been on with yogurt," Dixie hears herself saying. But they don't mind; they laugh.

Shane keeps weighing the panniers in his hands, making sure they're equal, because if one is even a pound or two heavier than the other, eventually the whole thing starts to slide off. Shane used to be an efficiency expert, walked around in a three-piece suit checking the way people did things. He must have looked like he does now, stern and important. Dixie might tell everyone later, when she gets to know them better, how Shane used to be an efficiency expert, how he's a college graduate and all.

That beer went right through her. She goes down into a draw behind some bushes to pee, and when she comes back, Shane's tied the whole thing on with a double diamond hitch.

"That's the part I needed to watch," she tells him.

"Well, you should've stayed up here, then. I can't hang around all day babysitting this bunch."

It's late when they camp at Elk Park. It's a really nice meadow with little streams running through and the ruin of a cabin—the humpback's cabin—among the pines. There isn't much left of the ruin, just a rectangle of stones where the foundation was and a small caved-in cellar. Over the years, campers must have used the timbers for their fires.

"Who owns this land?" Foster asks.

"No one. I mean, it's park, I think," Dixie says.

"Actually Marietta owns it," Lily tells Dixie. "Her father bought up big pieces of land before he opened the ski mountain. I guess we have to stop here. I wanted to camp at Lake Cora farther up, but we got started too late." She doesn't say it's Dixie's fault, but she's thinking it.

It's dark by the time they eat. It's a good thing Shane didn't come, because it's Italian rice with dried mushrooms—Meg's a vegetarian—and Shane always wants T-bones the first night out. Dixie shares some of their vodka, then opens a bottle of rum she brought. Foster plays the guitar, and after dinner they sing, everything from the Beatles to "Onward, Christian Soldiers." Foster and Meg sing on TV commercials. Dixie feels like they're trying to sell her something and she doesn't join in, but then she hears herself saying, "Do that John Denver song, 'Take Me Home, Country Roads,' " and of course she has to join in. She used to sing all the time, still does with Louis in the shop when they're working together.

The three women share the big tent and Foster sleeps alone in the small one. This surprises Dixie, because she assumed Foster would sleep with Meg. She asks Meg if Foster is "gay," that's the word they like you to use. Meg laughs so long that Dixie is beginning to get pissed off, then Meg explains that Foster is an old friend of hers who only a couple of weeks ago got separated from his wife. He has a little boy and he's been very depressed over the whole thing, so she persuaded him to come with her for a change of scene.

Dixie pulls on the rum a bit, which turns out to be a mistake, because then she feels sick and damned if she wants to get out of the bag and go puke in the cold. She sticks her head out of the tent. Stars swarm overhead. She tries to pick out the constellations but the stars won't stop buzzing around.

The next morning Dixie sends them up to the Divide without her. She'll stay back with the Appaloosa, let her fatten herself on the grass and rest for the trip down. Leave the tents, she tells them, the breakfast dishes. "I'll have everything washed and packed by the time you get back."

She doesn't want to deal with all that first thing in the morning. She wants them and their bustling energy out of the way. She isn't feeling that well. A beer settles her stomach some. She builds the fire high to warm her fingers and toes. It's going to be piss cold up on the Divide—wind and snow. She lays some of the horse blankets by the fire, puts her sleeping bag on top, and crawls in. The rum bottle is in the bottom of her bag. She pulls on that some. The packhorse nickers. Dixie loves being up in the mountains. Shane should have come, but if he were here, she wouldn't be lying at her ease drinking rum and watching clouds tumbling over the mountain. He'd have her washing up, getting things ready so he could pack. A trip into backcountry should be relaxing, but Shane just gets more intense.

When the snow starts she thinks it's ashes at first. Yesterday they were in T-shirts and today—that's the way it is in the mountains. Without leaving her bag, she reaches out to throw the last log on the fire. People have been trapped up here in snowfalls—hikers mainly, who don't understand how the weather can change suddenly. Up in the mountains you get a whole other kind of weather than what they're having in town.

She tries to picture Shane standing outside the trailer looking off toward Disappointment Pass, seeing the clouds gathering and feeling concerned that it might be snowing up where Dixie is. Instead, she sees him still wearing his clothes from the night before, sleeping in the middle of the bed with the torn sheet coming off one corner of the mattress.

She starts thinking about Louis, how he's taught her everything about upholstery, how he praises her. When she gets it wrong, he corrects her, but he never blames her or makes her feel stupid the way Shane does. Sometimes when they're working, they brush up against each other. It's mostly Dixie who brushes up against Louis, but she can tell he likes it. Louis is not interested in horses or having a ranch. You would never see him at the Lost Dollar. He works in his shop and goes upstairs at the end of the day, where he's fixed himself an apartment that Dixie's never had a chance to see. Even though he's a young man, this is probably all he'll ever do or want to do. Louis is content, but he has no dream; Shane has a dream, but it makes him mad all the time. Dixie surprises herself with this thought. She never compared Louis and Shane before. That's why it's good to get away in the mountains by yourself once in a while. It gives you a chance to think.

She must have dozed off without knowing it, because the next time she looks, the ground is completely white. The Appaloosa whinnies and is answered by distant horses. Dixie checks her watch and is amazed that three and a half hours have passed since the others left.

As soon as she crawls from the bag, she feels the effect

of the rum and the beer. She scrambles up the rocks behind the camp and squats in the snow. From up here the camp looks like something terrible happened and everyone rushed off, leaving dishes scattered by the fire, bedding spilling out of tents. Dixie said she'd have everything washed and packed by the time they came back, but they don't expect her to do all that, do they? It's too much for one person.

She's managed to roll up her own bag and stack the horse blankets under a tarp out of the snow when the others come in. They crowd around the fire.

"Is there any hot water, Dixie? I'm dying for a cup of tea," Lily says.

"We used it all for breakfast," Dixie says.

Foster is poking at the embers. "Where's all that wood we had? I had a whole stack of wood here—"

"There wasn't that much," Dixie says.

Foster opens his mouth to say something, but Lily interrupts. "Look, let's just get some water boiling and pack this stuff so we can get out of here. This snow's piling up pretty fast."

Lily takes the kettle to the stream for water. Foster goes for wood. Meg follows him. Dixie begins wiping off the breakfast dishes with paper towels.

Foster builds up the fire and helps Meg fold the tents. The water is taking its time getting to the boil. Foster already has the panniers packed by the time Dixie is able to call out, "Teatime, everyone!" She pours a little rum into everybody's cup and tosses the empty bottle in the pannier. They could use the rum; they're all walking around stiff-legged and quiet. No one meets her eyes. After tea, Dixie douses the fire and shovels dirt on top. She looks around the camp, all cleared of tents and dishes, sleeping bags, clothing. It wasn't such an impossible job after all.

"Dixie—" Lily's standing by the packhorse. The pan-

niers and sleeping bags have been loaded on. They've put
the tarp over it. "Can you give us a hand tying this on?
The double diamond hitch on top—nobody's sure how
that works."

"Are you sure these are the same ropes, 'cause they look
all different," Dixie says. The ropes could have gotten
mixed up in the packing. Everyone says they're the exact
same ropes Shane put on yesterday. Dixie goes around and
examines the ropes on the other horses. "Are you sure you
didn't pack up any extra rope," she asks. Foster looks at
Meg.

Dixie stands on a log and lays the ropes across the horse's
back. She knows they're supposed to go into a double
diamond hitch, but for the life of her she can't figure out
how. Everyone remembers some part. They get it tied on.
It doesn't look right, and the Appaloosa knows it isn't, but
everyone's in a hurry to ride down out of the snow, so
Dixie doesn't argue.

Simone, Lily's Arabian, has a short stride. Dixie mentions
it to Lily, who's just ahead on the mule.

"Yeah, I've got to work on her to lengthen her pace."

"How do you do that?"

"By taking her out on long trips like this, making her
walk, not letting her trot. She's my guest horse; I've let a
lot of different people ride her and they've spoiled her."

Dixie reins the Arabian in. "Slow down there," she says.
It's the first Lily has answered Dixie with anything more
than "Is that right?" since they started down. They talk
some more about the Arabian, her likes and dislikes, what
spooks her. They discuss whether she's "honest" or not, a
term Shane and his friends use when talking about horses.
Lily says Dixie's welcome to come ride Simone anytime,
that she'd be doing Lily a favor.

Up ahead, the Appaloosa is dancing all over the trail.

Foster, who has the lead rope, is talking to Meg and doesn't notice. Lily and Dixie call to Foster to pull in the rope. Then they see that the pack saddle is slipping off.

Dixie slides from her horse, gives the reins to Lily, and goes over to the Appaloosa. Everything stands out sharp and clear, the way it does after a storm. The odors of horse sweat, leather tackle, piney air hit her as if someone had just switched on her sense of smell. She and Foster take everything off the horse and lay it on the ground. She places the blanket, then the pack saddle, and straps it tight. The panniers hang from the saddle, the sleeping bags in the middle, and the tarp over that.

Now the ropes. Her mouth is dry. She considers getting a beer from her saddlebag, but the Arabian is far up the trail and all the horses are restless. She lays one rope across the front and her hands take over from there. She jumps on the log, pulls the rope up, twists it with the other. She's under the horse, over the horse, working like a crazy woman, doing it all before she loses it again. It looks great. Maybe not as good as Shane's, but it's right. Meg cheers.

"That was incredible, when you got it, when you suddenly *knew* how it went," Meg says. They're having vodka and cranberry juice. Foster's cooking spaghetti with spinach, black olives, and some kind of cheese, not spaghetti cheese. Dixie isn't having a drink. She had enough rum this morning. She doesn't want to go into that haze again.

The thing is, she tells Lily and Meg later in the tent, Shane never lets her pack the horse. He shows her part of it but never all. She's usually cooking or cleaning up. This was the first time she was ever allowed to pack a horse.

"Now that you've figured it out, you won't ever forget," Meg says.

Dixie pokes her head out of the tent. She just realized that they're going to expect her to pack that horse again tomorrow morning, now that she's proven she can do it. But she has the kind of brain where things get lost and she can't always find them when she needs to.

For instance, last night the stars were swarming in confusion and tonight they are laid out in constellations. There's Cassiopeia, the chair, and next to it Perseus, and over them Andromeda. That watery blob in Andromeda that looks like a mistake, like light trying to get itself together to make a star, is really a whole other galaxy with stars and planets, comets and meteors, whizzing around according to certain rules of physics, but going backward compared to the way our own galaxy, the Milky Way, is turning. Our galaxy and Andromeda are like twin whirlpools side by side, turning different ways.

Maybe her mind is like that—two separate parts, turning different ways. Most of the time, she lives with the fuzzy, jumbled, emotional side, but sometimes she makes the leap into a place where she sees clearly—everything from the way ropes go to the shape of constellations. She stares up at Andromeda, trying to concentrate, but she gets cold and her neck grows stiff. Before she knows it, she's back in the tent, asleep.

CHAPTER 5

■ ■ ■

Easy Keeper

FOSTER COLEMAN, now legally separated from his wife, joined by elaborate custody arrangements to his son, is flying alone to Priest Creek to spend a week with Lily. He barely knows her. The pack trip last fall was right after his separation when he was myopic with grief and guilt. He remembers only Lily's weathered skin, her long, straight, gray hair, and her way of listening a little too closely to whatever he said. He could stay in a hotel near the ski slope and invite Lily for a dinner or a day of skiing. It might be easier for both of them. But Foster has no skills for being alone—even in his own apartment. There's something about coming home to empty rooms that can force him out again for a beer, or sometimes to his mother's, where he sleeps in his boyhood bed. How much worse to be alone in a hotel room with only a TV and the sounds of strangers in the next room for company.

The plane from Denver to Priest Creek—a Dash 7 designed for short runways—rises sharply, then drops. The air seems filled with invisible mountains and valleys, barriers to the traveler, that make his stomach curdle and make him regret ever venturing here. Foster grips the armrest. It's typical of Meg to blithely send him off to this frozen, alien place for a week of awkward loneliness. They were supposed to be going together and at the last minute she was offered a job she couldn't turn down. She says she'll join him in a couple of days.

She suggested the trip one Monday when they were re-cording a commercial Foster had written for a new sham-poo. Foster was coming off a hellish weekend. He'd had to pick up Nicholas, his son, at nine on Saturday morning, and his Friday-night date, someone called Gemma Rose, had refused to go home. (Bella—his mother—says women with double names tend to expect too much.) He'd let Gemma Rose stay, thinking she'd be a help with Nicholas, but instead she competed with him for Foster's attention. He returned Nicholas Sunday evening, and at midnight Foster's ex-wife was on the phone screaming that Nicholas couldn't sleep—he'd been traumatized because Foster had a strange woman sleeping in his bed—and she was going to take Foster to court.

Meg said Foster looked awful and he said he didn't have any time for himself. Everyone wanted him, including his ex-wife, who wouldn't let go. You have to get away, Meg said.

When Lily meets him at the airport, Foster says, "I can get a room in a hotel." He feels he should offer this option. Meg said she'd join them as soon as the job was over, but knowing Meg, another job could come up that she couldn't refuse either and she could cancel the trip entirely.

"I like having someone else around the place. You can help me with the lambs." Lily motions for Foster to throw his bags in the back of a vintage Chevy pickup—it's got a white paint job that looks as though she did it herself. There's straw in the back of the truck, with what might be animal droppings mixed in. He lays his skis and bag, new and expensive, in the part of the straw that looks the freshest.

Lily raises sheep—Foster remembers now. On the pack trip he never focused on what she did, other than ride a mule with enviable authority. Now that he knows he will be staying alone with Lily, there are all kinds of questions he needs the answers to.

He opens the door and a large woolly dog rears up from the seat. "Gravy, get in the back," Lily says in a conversational tone. The dog leaps past Foster and scrabbles up next to the luggage.

Foster resists an impulse to brush off the seat before getting in. He looks for a seat belt; there isn't any. "So," he begins, "did you grow up here?"

"No."

"Oh really." When she doesn't reply, he adds, "How long have you lived here?"

"Since '70."

"Nineteen-seventy. About the time they opened the ski area?"

"That's right."

"Are you a big skier, then?"

"When there's time." She pulls into a feed-and-grain place. "Wait here," she says, jumping out.

She comes back carrying a large sack over her shoulder. He jumps out too, then hesitates. She might be the kind of woman who gets insulted when a man tries to help. Lily smiles and surrenders her bag. "Thanks," she says.

She's smaller than Foster remembered her, short and slight, but strong. The sack is heavy. Foster drops it onto the straw.

As Lily drives, Foster looks out at wintry hills, at long, unbroken drifts gleaming in the sun, and thinks of Nicholas, who has to make do with the bruised scraps of snow he finds in the park near home. "God, it's beautiful," he says. This is a poor substitute for the lament crouching in his throat.

"We had a ninety-inch base, but it's melting fast." She downshifts to get up a rutted mud road, her driveway. Animals—sheep? goats?—scatter before them. "My mouflons. It's an ancient breed from Sardinia. They jump over any fence I put up, so I don't bother trying. The breed is older than fences. It's okay. Everyone knows they're my sheep."

They pull up in front of an unpainted wooden house with an overhanging tin roof. There's a barn and sheds also built of weathered boards. These simple buildings, so harmoniously placed, make him yearn for something gone or for something that never was. "It's paradise," he says.

Lily has already jumped from the truck. "Take your stuff in, it isn't locked." She strides off to the barn, the sack across her shoulder.

Bella would say the house could stand a good dusting. There are stained-glass doors on the kitchen cabinets, pot-bellied stoves in the two sitting rooms that flank the central kitchen, hanging pots of ivy in macramé holders in the windows. Notices are stuck on the refrigerator door with magnets: fairs, mule-training groups, a sheep breeders' conference. The house feels like a meeting place, a hub, has none of the telltale signs of being a single person's lair. Foster checks the freezer and finds that it's filled with hand-labeled packages of meat, boxes of ice-cream pops, some Sara Lee cakes. He can imagine her pulling things out, preparing dinner for a crowd of friends who just happened to stop by.

Lily comes in, stamping snow off her boots, and catches him snooping in her freezer. "Try to keep this door closed; it saves heat," she says, and shuts the door between the kitchen and the mudroom.

Foster walks away from the refrigerator, feeling like a foolish, prying city boy. But she forgives him, with the ease of someone who's had a lot of practice. "There's a bottle of Colorado wine in the refrigerator and some Canadian Club, if you want a drink," she says. She's even smaller now without her parka and boots, but her voice is large and deep, an outdoor voice.

"Maybe I'll try the Canadian Club." Feeling Western, Foster pours himself a slug of whiskey over ice. "Can I fix one for you?"

She reaches past him to get a Coke out of the refrigerator. "It will just make me sleepy. I have the feeling I'm going to have to deliver a lamb before the night is out."

Foster grimaces as he tastes the whiskey. "I would have thought they could take care of that themselves."

"Sometimes I have to help. I've got a couple of first-time mothers out there. I might have to stand a newborn up, help it find the teat."

She pulls a casserole out of the refrigerator and places it on the stove. "Leftover shepherd's pie. The lamb's homegrown."

"You eat them?" A stupid question, he realizes, even as he says it. Somehow he'd thought Lily was raising sheep as pets or, vaguely, for the wool. He hadn't considered the end result of sheep raising.

She treats his question with more respect than it deserves, explains that she breeds sheep for the meat they produce. She usually sells the lambs to 4-H'ers to raise and show at fairs. The lambs are judged twice, once in the ring and once again after they've been slaughtered. "That's when you see how good the judge was, when you see the carcass. It's the final test."

Foster likes sitting at Lily's oak table while she puts dinner together and talks about sheep. He likes it that he can feel comfortable far from his usual environment. Of course, the whiskey is helping. He's always been attracted to country women. His wife grew up on a farm in West Virginia. There were five kids in her family, each one named after a different state. The names turned out to be prophecies: the children all left home as soon as they were able. It intrigued Foster that his wife, Dakota, hadn't seen her family in years, had completely lost track of two brothers. Foster, an only child, speaks to Bella daily over the phone, sees each of his parents (who amicably divorced after Foster left college) once a week. They're psychiatrists: Bella, a child therapist; Philip, a Freudian analyst. In Foster's family, moods were analyzed, differences talked out, consensus reached. In his wife's family, doors were slammed and people left for years without explanation.

Foster shows Lily a picture of Nicholas. She examines it under the light. "He doesn't look like you. The bone structure's different." Foster takes the picture back, a little diffidently. He's used to having women coo over pictures of Nicholas—his widely spaced eyes, his golden hair. Lily has judged him with a breeder's eye.

"He's more like his mother's side. They're from West Virginia."

"Is that right?" Lily sets the casserole on the table. Her forearms are enormous, like a man's, shocking on her slight body. Her hands are thick and calloused, with deep lines around the knuckles. She dishes up the lamb. "You should bring him next time. Kids love it here."

When she talks she looks directly into his eyes, which bothers him, because the conversation doesn't warrant prolonged eye contact. It makes him wonder what she sees or what she's looking for. Hers are practical eyes, used for spotting a stray sheep on the side of a hill or examining a cut in a horse's shin. They are not skilled in the sidelong glance, the quick downturn, the sly nuances that signal sexual attraction. Foster, on the other hand, is fluent in the language of courtship. He can usually predict in the first half hour whether an evening will end in bed or with a kiss at the door. He is rarely caught in an embarrassing misjudgment.

She eats quickly, efficiently, and then jumps up and says, "Oh, I'd better show you your room."

"Don't bother, just tell me—"

"I'd better look. I can't remember if there are sheets and towels. Bring your stuff."

At first Foster feels a twinge of disappointment when he sees that his room is on the other side of the house from hers. Separate stair, separate bath. But no, it's refreshing, he tells himself—a much needed vacation to live this way with a woman, if only for a week. He'll help out. He'll be a friend, the perfect guest. "This room is great," he says. "Let me know if I can help you. I don't want to be in the way here."

Later, washing dishes while Lily goes to the barn, Foster tells himself Meg was right after all. He did need to get away. Already he's breathing more freely. It amuses him to be left in the kitchen while Lily's pitching hay or whatever. Role reversal is restful once in a while. Maybe Lily will take the initiative. He imagines her wiry thighs clasped around his waist and spills too much detergent into the water, making billows of bubbles. Lily cautioned him against using too much soap because of the septic system. He turns the spigot on full blast and manages to get it all down the drain before she returns. A little news on the television and they are ready for bed—Lily because she'll be up in the night with a first-time mother she's certain will give birth, Foster because he's still on New York time. Lily promises to wake him early to teach him some chores. Foster lays warm clothes beside his bed in anticipation, and then in the middle of the night—2:12, his watch says—he finds himself pulling these clothes on, hurrying downstairs, grabbing his boots and parka, all because Lily touched his shoulder and told him to come to the barn.

The cold stuns him. He forgets to breathe. All around

him stars—thousands of them—flicker red, blue, yellow. These are not the sparse remote blobs Foster sees far overhead in the city when he sometimes points out the Big Dipper to Nicholas. In this sky, stars look like what they are, great boiling fires of heaven.

"Foster!" Lily calls from the barn. Suddenly Foster is fully awake. Lily has summoned him and he has come, but inside the barn, his stomach does a slow roll. The palms of his hands, the soles of his feet, prickle with an urge to crawl away.

His wife insisted that Foster be present at their son's birth. They went to Lamaze class together. He learned so many ways to help—timing contractions, pressing tennis balls into her lower back—but when the actual labor arrived, she wouldn't let him do anything but watch, helpless witness to her agony, and all the while she cursed him for putting her through it. She said words he'll never forget, couldn't repeat, even to Bella. The doctor placed a scrubbed pink hand on Foster's shoulder afterward and said he was concerned, what was the story with his wife, had she wanted the child, would she be able to care for it?

"Foster!"

The smells of sheep dung and straw thicken in his throat. The barn is dark except for the light of one bare bulb hanging over a pen of chicken wire and the red glow of a space heater. Lily has thrown her parka to one side and she is anointing her hands and forearms with Crisco oil. "She's having problems. I'm going to have to help her. If you could just hold her still from the front—"

The ewe is staring dully. Her back legs are rigid, stiffly spread. Foster looks away from the opening. He's never touched a sheep before, much less held one still. He places his hands where Lily tells him and kneels close. They don't bite, do they?

Lily's arm is deep inside the ewe. She shuts her eyes. The

animal heaves and shudders. Lily murmurs. Foster presses into the shoulders. A convulsive wave and Lily draws her arm forth. Grasped in her hand, the bloody thing, the lamb. "Good girl, good girl," Foster says, stroking the ewe, embracing her. His face is wet with tears.

Lily lays the lamb on the straw so its mother can lick it clean. All business, quick, efficient; but she smiles at Foster. "Push her head down," she says. Foster guides the ewe's head to her lamb and she begins to lick. Lily tugs gently on the umbilical cord that still connects the mother to the lamb.

"Don't you have to cut it?" Foster asks.

"She'll bite it off, if she's good."

They watch the ewe for a while. Foster actually feels proud when she bites the cord. He pats her neck. She shudders and the afterbirth plops out onto the straw. Lily cleans the ewe's rump, then picks up the afterbirth and lays it down beside the lamb.

"What are you doing?"

"I want her to eat the afterbirth. It's good for her."

"You sure?"

"They do that, the good mothers. It's nourishing." She coaxes the ewe toward the red mess. Foster looks away.

Lily finishes wiping down the lamb, wraps it in a towel, and holds it close to warm it. She does this casually, expertly. Foster remembers how the nurse wrapped and held Nicholas in a tight football-size bundle and how his body would jerk and flail in the amateur arms of Foster or his wife.

"Want to hold it?"

Before Foster can explain that he's really not very good at this sort of thing, the lamb is in his arms, bony and light. The heart beats fast against his hand. Then Lily takes the lamb from Foster and holds it against its mother. The lamb wavers. Its legs splay, then right themselves. Lily puts the teat in its mouth. It butts its head against the maternal belly. The ewe dances. Lily pats her neck and talks to her in soothing sounds.

Something bleats in the dark beyond the circle of light over the pen. They are surrounded by other ewes and lambs, shifting, nursing, witnessing. Births have been going on routinely in this barn almost every night, sometimes twice in one night. Foster feels giddy as though he's come through something dangerous. He wants to see it again, wants Nicholas to see it.

The ewe catches a few mouthfuls of straw while her lamb suckles. New mother, new lamb. The instinct has kicked in and they're acting like old pros. Lily rakes up the bloodied straw and puts down fresh, all the while explaining how she matched a ram from a breed that produces a large percentage of lean meat with this female, who's an easy keeper.

"Easy keeper?"

"They don't take as much feed as the others for the amount of meat they produce." Lily rubs the ewe between the ears. The lamb's ropy tail switches back and forth.

"I like the term, easy keeper."

"You never heard it before?"

"No."

On a recent afternoon at Bella's, Foster accused his mother of having managed too well when he was growing up. "It seemed so easy, the way you two got along, the way I fit into your marriage. It ran so smoothly that I never had to think about how it worked." Bella said it seemed easy to her too. It was only after Foster left for college that she realized how hard it was.

Lily has straw in her hair and blood on her parka, but she doesn't mind. Foster follows her out of the barn, already imagining how her hips will feel in his hands. He knows she will let him share her bed, as easily as she served him the stew, as easily as she delivered the lamb. He already knows how simple it will be and how they will fall asleep immediately afterward. The air is cold and smells of snow and faintly of iron forged millions of years ago in distant stars. He fills his lungs, fills his brain with oxygen to burn away memories of a marriage over at last.

CHAPTER 6

■ ■ ■

Bibleback Ridge

Driving out of town on Mine Road, you'll see a ridge on your right. It was named for an early homesteader who had a deformity, one Bibleback Burton, because the ridge resembled the hump on his back. Bibleback was a dark figure in the history of Priest Creek, and that might account for some of the unfortunate accidents that have occurred around there, as well as for the eerie green light that sometimes appears over the ridge shortly after sunset.

—from the Priest Creek *Crier*

MEG CALLS LILY midweek to say she won't be coming out after all. She finished her job, but she has to rerecord something she did a while ago—not her fault, the technicians, but what can she do? How are you and Foster getting along? she asks.

"Oh fine. He helps with the chores . . . No, no skiing yet, but the snow isn't very good. We could use one big storm or they're going to have to shut down the mountain early—"

"How are you getting along, you and Foster?" Meg persists.

"He asks a lot of questions. I feel like I'm being inter-viewed all the time."

"Poor Foster. He must feel so out of place there. He's a real city boy. Is he going to be mad that I'm canceling out?"

Lily looks at Foster chopping onions at the kitchen counter. "I think he's having a good time."

"Where's he sleeping?"

"Well, with me."

They both laugh.

Foster looks up from his chopping. "She isn't coming. I knew she wouldn't."

"She says she hopes you're not angry."

Foster transfers the onions to the skillet. "Happy. You know how cheap Meg is. She'd have me skiing every day to get her money's worth out of the plane ticket. I like just hanging here with you. I needed you, and your place. In the city I'm dancing on laser beams all the time. I get so I can't connect, even with my own son sometimes."

He's so unguarded that she feels embarrassed for him. He says it right out: I need you. She would not say these words to him.

Last fall on the pack trip, Meg said that Lily should find a man, anyone as long as he was decent, just to help her get over Jerry. Lily said there was someone she liked but she didn't want to risk losing him as a friend by taking him as a lover. That good-old-boy who rented his fat horses to them? Meg asked. Surely Lily could do better.

Lily watches Foster stirring the sauce. His sleeves are rolled up; the hairs on his forearms gleam golden in the light. Although his hair is dark, she can tell he was blond as a boy—blond and blue-eyed. He's small-boned, around five nine, and is well developed, in that perfect-proportioned, almost artificial way that people are who work out, as opposed to just work. He's been a helpful guest, and entertaining—he can talk circles around Lily, but then she's not a word person. Lily wonders if Meg realized that she was sending Foster to Lily almost exactly a year after Jerry died. Meg's well-intentioned but careless.

"Do you have any Parmesan?" Foster asks.

"Spaghetti cheese? Sure." She ducks into the pantry and finds the Kraft cheese in the shaker, the large size. He handles it as if it were an artifact. "They're still making these. Amazing. Next time I'll bring you real Parmesan. There's an Italian cheese store near me. I have them cut it off the wheel."

Lily won't permit herself to blame Meg. After all, Lily could have chosen to let Foster stay in a hotel—he offered. She could have decided not to call him in the middle of the night to see the birth. She hesitated for a moment at the foot of the stairs. She knew she was at a juncture from which events could lead one way or the other, but she went to his room anyway and touched his sleeping shoulder.

"You're looking at me the way you look at your sheep, trying to figure out how much meat's on the bone," Foster says.

Evelyn, Lily's mother, calls while they're having dinner.

"Goddamn Minny. You have to get me a new girl, Lily. This one can't do shit with my hair . . ."

Lily holds the receiver away from her ear. "Mom . . . Mom . . . Mom, let me talk to Minny. Put Minny on the phone . . . All right, Mom. Let me talk to her."

She can hear them struggling. Before Lily hired Minny as a companion for her mother, there would sometimes be five phone calls a day—her mother would forget she had called. Now Lily phones her mother every Sunday morning and Evelyn is not supposed to call. Minny understands this, but she says that Evelyn got to the phone while Minny was doing laundry. Evelyn's sneaky—weak and helpless except when she wants to do something she shouldn't. Minny says she doesn't know how much longer she can put up with her.

"That was your mother?" Foster asks when Lily hangs up.

"Yes."

"You sounded annoyed."

"I was."

"It's not like you to *sound* annoyed. I think you get impatient with people but you control it at the source. You forgive before you blame."

"Is that right?"

Foster laughs. "That's one of the things you say when you're annoyed."

Lily stops herself from saying, "Is that right?"—something she never realized she said.

"Does she live nearby?" Foster asks.

"Who?"

Foster gives her a look.

"Oh, my mother. No."

"Where does she live?"

"Palm Beach."

"You're kidding! How did your mother come to live in Palm Beach? That isn't where you grew up, is it? Palm Beach?"

"She moved there when my father died." Lily gets up and takes her plate to the sink. "That was real good. I better go check on the lambs."

The next day, Lily is pitching straw into the pens where the newborn lambs and their mothers are. Foster barges in, banging the door behind him. "That goddamn turkey's after me. I swear it's personal. He goes right for my balls and he struts around you, preening, showing off his tail.

He's got some mad Leda and the Swan delusion going on there. I wouldn't turn my back on him if I were you."

Lily hands him the pitchfork. "See this pen? You can do the other way I did this one, if you want."

Trot, standing outside the door, is the last of the turkeys. The others have been sacrificed for various holidays. Trot doesn't know it but he's about to become the main dish at her pre-Easter party. Or maybe he does and is taunting her to get it over with. She sharpens her knife in the kitchen and stuffs some rope in her pocket. Trot is waiting with angry red eyes. He races her to the clothesline. He whoops when she catches him by his legs. His wings beat her while she twists the rope around and strings him to the line. Then he is still, confused by the novelty of hanging upside down. Blood fans out over the ground while Trot, headless on the line, twitches and spreads his wings, nerves sending crazy signals to his muscles, a synapse blizzard. The severed head questions the sky.

"You didn't have to kill him." Foster, pale, his eyes wide and dark, has been watching. Lily looks at her red hands, her knife.

All day clouds pile up in the southwest. There's a storm coming from New Mexico, bringing a foot of snow, maybe two, they're saying. It begins at night when Lily and Foster are in the hot tub. "You should go skiing tomorrow in the fresh powder," she tells him. "Why stay around to party with people you don't know?"

"I can't get the hang of powder skiing. I keep falling. Anyway, I want to meet your friends."

"We'll talk about the weather and how the price of land is going up. It's not going to be very interesting for an outsider."

"Unless you don't want them to see me, to know that you have a man staying with you."

"They knew about you the minute your plane landed."
She climbs out to get a Pacifico from the snowbank where
she's been keeping it cold.

"This hot tub's been here awhile," Foster says.

"It's an old wine barrel. We put it in when we built the
deck. It was Jerry's idea. I hadn't even heard of hot tubs."

"Jerry was your husband."

"Right."

"This is the first you've even mentioned his name to me."
Lily gets back in and hands the beer to Foster.

"I guess you're not going to talk about him," he says
after a while. They share the beer while snow falls in heavy
flakes around them. "Look at that!" Foster is pointing to
the edge of the light where her Manx ram, Jake, is pa-
trolling. "It's a unicorn."

Silhouetted against the light, with only one conical horn
showing, he does suggest a unicorn. "That's old Jake," Lily
says. "I really should put a bullet through his head, except
his meat would be stringy and tough. He's not doing his
job. Didn't mount one ewe last season."

"How do you know that? He might do it behind a bush.
He might be exceptionally modest."

Lily explains how she puts belts with markers on her
rams, a different color for each one. When a ram mounts
a ewe, he leaves a stripe of color on her rump.

"You've got a little kingdom here, don't you," he says.
"You have the power of life and death and procreation.
You have a castle in the snow guarded by unicorns and
amorous fowl."

"You have some imagination," she says.

Snow is coming down hard in the morning. The sheep are
huddled in the lee side of the barn, even the tough little
mouflons. Lily pitches hay to them. They nibble at her
parka. She brushes snow off their backs. Foster has finished

his chores and is building a rabbit out of snow as a surprise for the children who will be coming to the party. "This is fantastic. The packing's great!"

Later, she hears him on the phone with his son. "Man, you should see the snow out here! It's over your head! . . . Next year you'll come out with me and we'll build a —what? . . . Yeah, a dinosaur. That'll be cool. A snow dinosaur. You can meet my friend Lily and she'll show you her lambs and you can watch her milk a goat . . . Sure she does!" As Foster talks, Lily sees herself through his eyes —a woman on a ranch in Colorado who will always be here to receive Foster and his rapidly growing son.

Foster makes the stuffing for the turkey. "I like to cook. I used to love it when our housekeeper was off on weekends and I could help my mother. It was only BLT's or omelets or something like that. Bella's no chef." Foster wants to exchange pasts, presents, futures, everything they can in the week they have together. He tells her stories about his son, his mother, and even his ex-wife, with such ease that Lily's come to suspect he has told the stories many times. He has perfected and polished them so that they are smooth in his mouth and cause him no pain. He expects Lily to give him her stories in return, but she would have to fashion them from feelings she's never clothed in words. If she did this—and she isn't sure Foster would have the patience or fortitude to listen—Foster himself would be mixed in with the telling. The story is altered by the listener. In that way, Foster would insinuate himself into her past as well as her present.

The party begins around five o'clock, Saturday night. There's a buffet in the kitchen. The adults eat and drink. The children color eggs and eventually get whiny and have to be taken home. Through it all, every time Lily looks around, Foster is talking to someone else. He's creating a buzz, changing the air around him. Rather than being bothered by his questions, her friends can't seem to get enough.

Dusty arrives late. He hands Lily some loaves of braided sweet bread. "I had to help dig out two kids who got trapped in an avalanche up behind the hot springs," he says.

"Avalanche! You're kidding," Foster says.

Dusty studies Foster for a moment. "No, I'm not. There was three feet of snow on top of them. Happens sometimes up there. It's under a cliff. You get fresh snow on top of frozen—it will slide right down." They were two young men who work at Ski Town. Dusty knew them slightly, had had some beers with them at the Howling Coyote once. They were still alive, at least when they pulled them out.

"Why couldn't they get out themselves? Three feet of snow isn't that deep." Foster again.

"That stuff's like cement. You can't move. They were lucky—or knew enough—to keep a breathing space. One of them lost a glove. That's how we suspected someone was in there. We saw the glove on top."

Talk turns to the time a whole family on snowmobiles was overtaken by an avalanche at Bibleback Ridge. Dusty says he wouldn't go up to the ridge even in the summer.

"Why not?" Foster asks.

"Because it's cursed."

Talk stops. Someone snickers—Shane maybe. He and Dixie have just come in and are stowing a six-pack in the refrigerator.

Foster smiles. "I remember you. You're the guy with the horses, Death Wish I and II. Those were some pretty dangerous animals. It's a wonder you let them out to inexperienced riders. They actually broke into a trot. It was at the end, when they saw the parking lot."

"You were able to control them, were you?" Dusty moves past Foster to get a beer. Maybe there isn't a curse, he says, maybe there's nothing to it. But there are stories about the ridge, and there is that green light sometimes, after sunset.

"You'll see better when the moon comes up," Lily calls to Foster. She stops to let him catch up at the top of the rise, where there's a break in the pines and a view across the valley to the next range of mountains. This is Foster's last night. She was going to take him downhill skiing today, but she had some problems with a lamb and they never got out, so she fitted him with Jerry's old cross-country skis, packed food and drink in knapsacks, and drove to Bibleback Ridge to watch the moon rise.

A year ago, on this day, Jerry died. She hasn't told Foster this, but as she was pushing her way across the snow, she found herself having a conversation with Foster in her mind, explaining how it was with Jerry, how because the ranch had cured him once, she continued to expect that it would again, that the time would come around, like a season of the year. She watches Foster laboring up the last rise, losing momentum with each step, dissipating his energy.

"Is this where we eat, I hope?" He throws his pack down.

"Don't go near the edge. It could be just snow with nothing under it," she warns.

Foster backs away fast, trips on his ski, and falls at her feet. "It's not funny," he says, which only makes her laugh harder.

"I'm sorry. You looked funny for a minute there."

"Yeah, I guess I did." Foster lets her help him up.

They eat turkey left over from the party, washed down with beer and peppermint schnapps. Lily points to the glow in the sky where the moon will appear. She's waiting for him to ask her something about Jerry—all week, he's been relentless, if gentle, in his probings on the subject—but Foster wants to talk about avalanches. It fascinates him that one could have occurred right in town. (The boys are alive, but one had to have part of a leg amputated; the other lost some toes.)

"It's interesting that you live with this danger and you are almost oblivious to it," he says.

"We know it's there. There are places we wouldn't go after a snowfall."

"If you got caught in an avalanche, what would you do?" Foster asks.

"I don't think there's much you can do. You just try to avoid getting in the situation."

He takes a swig of the schnapps. "That's an answer no one in New York would accept. If there were avalanches in New York City, there would be avalanche-preparedness classes you could go to."

After a week spent fitting himself into her life, today Foster has been drawing distinctions, telling her how the people in Priest Creek (and Lily) are different from the people in New York (and Foster). Whenever Lily went into the house, it seemed that Foster was on the phone to New York, arranging his work schedule for next week.

Suddenly the moon is there—massive, white as a bone, so close it seems to be rising from a hole in the ground. "Incredible," Foster says. "We never see the moon rise in the city."

"I'm glad you know where we're going, because I can't see a damn thing." Foster is following her through the lodgepole pines where the branches block the light. She's been letting her feet find the way and hasn't worried over whether or not it's how they came in. She can get her bearings when they reach the clearing. Foster's questions have stopped. There was no opportunity to tell him about Jerry. She was careful not to tell him her stories too soon, but he was too impatient to wait. He invented her. He'll take back his own stories about her—how she killed a turkey, raises sheep that look like unicorns—stories that preserve her like a smooth hard pebble, a souvenir, something he can take out and show his friends.

He, on the other hand, inundated her with his stories of Foster, and yet he is leaving her with less than nothing, with empty spaces—at the kitchen counter, in the hot tub, in her bed—absences, abscesses, all over her home. He is leaving her mind echoing with stories she never told.

When they emerge from the trees, it seems as bright as day. The snow reflects the colorless light of the moon, creating a landscape of white spaces and black shapes. They chase their own elongated forms across the clearing. "Moon shadows. I can't remember when I've seen moon shadows," Foster says.

Lily stops, takes the last beer out of the pack, and hands it to him. "I guess that ridge could look like the hump of a man's back, but I don't see any of that spooky green light Dusty was talking about," she says.

"You don't mean this is the place where the snowmobilers disappeared."

Lily's sure she mentioned it to Foster, that they were going to Bibleback Ridge, but apparently she hadn't.

"We could have been killed," he says.

"Not on this side." She finishes the beer and stows the can in her pack. There's a thud behind them, maybe some snow falling from a tree. Lily looks up to see Foster skiing very fast in a direct line to the road.

"Hey! The truck's over this way!" she calls, but he doesn't stop or even acknowledge that he's heard. He's walking along the road, skis over his shoulder, when she picks him up in the truck.

"Where did you think the snow would come from?" she asks. "We were on flat ground. Snow doesn't rise up and swallow you."

He dumps the skis in the back and hops in beside her. "Yeah, I know. Once I started I couldn't stop, even though I knew I looked ridiculous and you were laughing at me. I had to make it to the road. It was as if my life depended on it."

"I told you avalanches happen on the other side of the ridge. We were never in any danger."

"Yeah. Well, you understand all that. There aren't any avalanches in the city, so it's completely strange to me. It's fear of the unknown, that's when you panic, when you don't understand the danger."

"And when you find out, it's too late," Lily says.

CHAPTER 7

■ ■ ■

Devil's Thumb

Devil's Thumb is the relic of an extinct volcano, the sides of which have washed away, leaving the harder lava core, or plug. The Utes named the upright cylindrical formation after a part of the male anatomy. Brides were encouraged to sleep in its moon shadow before their nuptials to ensure fertility.

White settlers prudishly renamed it a thumb and attributed it to the Devil, either because it was red or because they secretly thought it looked like what the Utes had named it originally.

Bibleback Burton claimed his mind took a dark turn after he camped nearby. If you go to see it, plan to leave before nightfall.

—from the Priest Creek *Crier*

DIXIE MOVES THE CUSHION off the bench in the dinette and props it against the cinder-block steps to the trailer so she can lie in the sun. It snowed a couple of days ago and now it could be summer, it's so hot. If you don't like the weather wait a bit and it will change—that's what they say around here.

Jewel is nosing around the garbage bins behind the Safeway. "Jewel, get out of there!" Dixie calls. Jewel comes over, tail wagging, and has a drink from a little puddle of melted snow that is forming at the edge of the cushion. Dixie pushes her back. The water's probably full of salt or whatever they spread on parking lots.

Dixie is reading a Treat Redheart book she borrowed over at Lily's Easter party last night. It was the first time she'd ever been invited to one of Lily's parties and she had planned to bake a lamb cake and decorate it with coconut, something she used to do back home in Florida, but things got away from her and she ended up taking Lily a six-pack of Pacifico and a bag of jellybeans.

The thing about Treat Redheart's books is they are all different but all the same, set in the Old West, when there were Indians, outlaws, bounty hunters. And they are authentic. You won't find even a weed growing where it shouldn't. That's what everyone says is good about the books, their authenticity. What Dixie likes is their certainty. She knows for instance that, in this book, Adam McCrae, a good man who's had hard luck all his life, will end up getting married to Harriet Dunroe, an independent woman of twenty-eight, who's had plenty of suitors but has turned them all down because she'd rather stay single than marry the wrong man. You can watch them moving toward each other and you know that however many Indian war parties, bounty hunters, or wrong men and women cross their paths, the two of them (he might be wounded—almost certainly will be—in the course of protecting her) will end up together. That's why Dixie keeps going back to Redheart like a healing spring.

"What the fuck are you doing?" Shane leans out the door, bare-chested, with his jeans, boots, and hat on. He's just gotten out of bed.

"I'm reading in the sun. What's it look like to you?"

"Like you're going to ruin that cushion in the wet."

"It's covered in waterproof vinyl. I should know, I did

it myself." It was her peace offering to Shane when she came back after things didn't work out with Louis. Louis gave her the vinyl, left over from a job they did for a pizzeria up in Ski Town.

"Lying out like that, you make the place look like trash."

"What, are you on the beautification committee or something?"

You would never find this conversation in one of Treat Redheart's books. It is not Shane's usual thing to worry over what the place looks like—a rented trailer behind the Safeway where the only neighbor is Frankie Delaney, who isn't right in the head. Events such as this conversation that don't fit and don't make sense are always coming up. Which is why her life isn't working out.

"That another Redheart? You must've swiped it over at Lily's."

"Borrowed."

"Why don't you make some coffee at least? You just flop down with a book like you're at a resort."

"Don't worry. I know I'm not at any resort."

Shane has a new attitude she doesn't like at all, that she should be doing chores, earning her keep, even though she already pays half the rent. When she came back from Louis's, Shane changed the rules.

Going to Louis was a mistake. She sees that now, how she forced it. If it was meant to be, it should have just happened, like in a Redheart novel.

Redheart's picture is on the back. From his face and neck you can tell he's heavy, probably short, and, although he wears a straw cowboy hat, certainly bald. Without the hat he would look like a laughing Buddha. Dixie sees him looming fat and smiling over the mesas and canyons, his short blunt fingers moving McCrae nearer and nearer to Harriet. That's how she should have gone to Louis, like an invisible hand was moving her.

She set the cups on the table. Her hands were strong, capable of chopping wood or hauling water, but they were gentle, the hands of a wife or mother. When McCrae looked at them, something went quiet inside him . . .

"Are you going to make that coffee or what?" Shane shoves the cushion with his boot.

Harriet wouldn't stand for anyone shoving her cushion. Redheart heroes know when to fight and when to walk away, but Dixie most of the time lets her mood decide, which is wrong. On this sunny Easter morning, with Jewel wanting her breakfast anyhow, it seems easiest just to make the coffee. Dixie hauls herself off the cushion, stretches, lifts her hair back from her shoulders. As she goes by, she brushes Shane with her hip.

Shane used to boil coffee and water in a big pot, cowboy-style, and then Dixie bought the automatic coffeemaker at Cashman & Sons. Shane called it a waste of money, but she's noticed he doesn't boil his coffee anymore.

"Shit! We're out of milk," Shane says.

Dixie nudges him out of the way to look in the refrigerator. There's a jar of pickles, some marshmallows left over from she's forgotten when, a can of Pacifico, and a piece of pizza that should be thrown out, but nothing she can use for milk.

"If you'll stop bitchin' for a minute I'll run over to the Safeway and get you some. I'm out of dog food too."

"See if you can score some of those wholewheat doughnuts so long as you're going."

Harriet and McCrae wouldn't run out of milk, because they'd have a ranch with a milk cow (a dream they both hold separately but haven't confided to each other). Dixie wants even less, a cabin with maybe an acre, enough for a few animals. She's wanted it ever since she headed out from Florida, but she hasn't been steadfast enough. If you get an image of your goal and think about it every day, eventually you will attain it. It's called Creative Imaging. She believes in it and knows it has worked for lots of people, but things get busy and she gets distracted and forgets to image. The reason she came to Colorado in the first place was to cancel out the mistakes of the past and begin living her life according to plan. She was even born by mistake, as her mother and grandmother were always ready to remind her, meaning she'd better behave because she was living under her grandparents' roof and, even on this earth, only as an uninvited guest. In later years, when her father would come to take her home to his new family for a visit in the summer, she had to help her stepmother with the babies and she always felt she was part of that family not by right but because she was useful.

One day, in tenth-grade biology, Miss Spencer pulled down a chart that had been hanging rolled up on the wall since the beginning of the year. It showed the development of the human embryo. Dixie saw how the little ball of cells grew, then folded in on itself and began developing a head and body, hands, eyes, mouth, all in perfect order. For the first time she saw that although her mother and father had made a mistake, Dixie herself had come together perfectly according to plan. It gave her hope. Of course she made mistakes after that. She should have gone to college; she shouldn't have married Bruce, but at least she'd been able to leave Bruce behind her and get out here where she could work on the plan for the rest of her life.

Shane is lying on the cushion, reading her book and smoking a cigarette.

"It's pretty good, isn't it?"

"They're all alike. Did you get the doughnuts?"

Dixie hands him the doughnuts and goes in for the coffee. Jewel is waiting patiently by her dish.

When Dixie first knew him, Shane used to talk about buying some land out on Conners Creek Road, where Lily lives. He said the trailer was only temporary, until he could get the down payment on a place together. And the trailer did look like an arrangement he'd made for only a month or two. His clothes were in duffels under his bed and his saddle was just inside the door, waiting for a horse. After Dixie moved in, she bought some secondhand furniture, a dresser and a couple of chairs. She sewed curtains for the windows. Maybe she shouldn't have.

"Doesn't that book make you want to saddle up some old pony and go riding up to the Divide and sleep out under the stars?" Dixie hands Shane his coffee.

Shane stirs it with his doughnut. "I'll be doing that soon enough, I guess. Jim Cosby says they're going to need an extra wrangler over at Eden Glen."

"I mean just us. I could get a few days off."

"In this mud and snow—"

"Later, in June."

"They got all those flies that time of year."

"We could go up anyway, do some fishing . . ."

But with all those flies it might not be so great. In July the mosquitoes are terrible. The best time is August, when Shane will be working at Eden Glen. "Maybe you could score me a gig as a cook and I could go with you."

"They got cooks." Shane wipes his hands on his jeans and rolls another cigarette. He picks up the book again.

"Excuse me. I think I was reading that." She plucks it from him and goes inside.

It's colder in than out, dark, and smells like old sheets. She could wash the sheets, but who wants to spend Easter morning in the Coin-Op, which is probably closed anyway.

She opens all the windows and takes the quilt off the bed so she can curl up under it while she reads on the couch.

He led her to a place where she could see the canyon and the steep trails leading up. He told her she might have to wait for hours, all day and possibly all night too. If an Apache came up this side of the canyon she had to be prepared to kill him. Could she do it?

She took the rifle from him. Her hands were pale but steady.

It was McCrae who trembled, not visibly but inside, to think that those hands might have to kill. He hoped he would live to see them again.

"Goodbye, then. If I'm not back by noon tomorrow, lead your horse down the back and head for Soda Flats. I have a friend at the saloon there, Shorty Stone. He'll take care of you."

She murmured her thanks, but he was already gone, silent as an Indian. She wondered if she'd ever see him alive again.

Dixie hears the refrigerator door opening and closing, and then the outside door slams shut. By the time she gets to the door, Shane's pickup is pulling onto the road. The cushion is still there. She pours another cup of coffee and takes her book out to the sun.

Shane sits in his truck looking at the Lost Dollar, its one dusty window with the unlit neon sign that says Coors, the fake-stone asbestos siding peeling by the door. It looks as if it has been closed since the last cowboy staggered out after drinking himself soggy to make up for two dry months on the range, or since the last grizzled prospector came down from Poverty Basin and announced there wasn't enough gold up there to fill a tooth with. But in fact it was open last night and will open again today. Not for a while, because it's Easter. Why is he here? He pulls the tab on a can of Pacifico he brought from home.

Ever since she came back it seems he's always driving off—so he won't have to look at her, her sloppiness, the way she doesn't care. And when she was at Louis's, he wasn't home much either, because he would start kicking furniture and breaking things. Either way he spent most of the winter in his truck or at the Lost Dollar.

What was his life like before she infected it? He can't remember, so it must have been okay. He doesn't even know how he got mixed up with her, just that one morning he woke up and she was in bed with him. She got up and started fixing breakfast as if it was the regular thing to do—didn't even ask where anything was. They must have struck a bargain at the Lost Dollar the night before, one he couldn't recall the terms of.

He'd heard of her before he saw her—a flake who'd come to town with a goat and some pet snakes in her car. There are plenty of that type coming and going. Priest Creek attracts them, and sooner or later they all show up at the Lost Dollar. When Dixie did, he was surprised she was so young and cute. She was little (that was before she got lardy in the thighs). She had a Southern accent—still does, especially after a couple of beers. Lately she's been trying to talk like Lily, who's her idol.

She'd never been out West before; she'd never known a cowboy. She perched on the barstool and her eyes shone when he mentioned five-foot rattlers lying across the trail or the time they had to go up to the Divide and rescue a group that had gotten lost in a snowstorm. Now she's heard all his stories. He tosses the empty can and heads up Canyon Road toward Devil's Thumb. He parks in the turnout where some hiking trails begin and gets out to piss away the beer. The view surprises him. It always does. He forgets what it does to him until he's here and sees the land, un-marked for miles, with a few ranches tucked in beside frozen creeks, looking the way it might have a hundred years ago. He breathes deeply. The air up here can wash out your soul. He kicks over the yellow place, making it white again.

He goes back to the truck and twists off the wire that holds the glove compartment shut and fishes out a poem he's been working on.

> A cowboy sits astride his steed,
> His heart is proud and free.
> Although his work is hard and long
> There's nothing he'd rather be.

At first it sounds even better than he remembered, but on second reading he isn't sure if "his heart" might not be taken to mean the horse's heart. He could change "steed" to "mare," but he likes the way "steed" works with "free" and "be."

When Shane was thirteen, he won a Fourth of July poetry contest and got a twenty-five-dollar prize. For about a year after that he wrote a lot of poems, and then he forgot about it, but a cowboy poetry contest in the Priest Creek *Crier* brought it all back. It was the prize money that got him started, but now he likes the way writing poetry takes his head to a different place, especially when he works out here. Last week he had to run the engine to keep warm, but today the sun is pouring in, heating his thighs so he can almost feel the horse under him.

Shane threw away his watch when he quit work as an efficiency expert, so he can't tell how long he's been asleep. The pines are casting purple shadows, and Devil's Thumb stands out red against the fir-covered mountains behind.

It's an effect that is caused by the setting sun, the rays slanting at an angle and bringing out the reds. Shane learned about this in physics, but he can't recall the name for it.

He feels a drawing on his insides, a sadness he can't explain. He's remembering a story Dusty told him in the Lost Dollar, about some poor sucker who lived a hundred years ago, a man who was born with a twisted back. Then Shane realizes he was dreaming about Ginny, his ex-wife. He married her because she was pregnant and he couldn't see himself telling her to get an abortion. It wasn't the kind of man he wanted to be, although he wouldn't have minded if she had just quietly gone off and had it done and told him afterward. So he married her. Then the baby was born three months early with a membrane around its lungs and died the next day. Soon after that, Shane just quit everything, Ginny, his job, and headed west. It's the part of his life he doesn't tell anyone. Dixie knows. He told her once and she said it was understandable, that he needed to leave the old life behind, that it was too messed up to fix. The only solution was to start new.

His poem is no good. He sees that now, reading it again. He strikes a match and holds the poem over the flame. The ash floats out the open window. It's a good thing he realized the poem was lousy before he spent a lot of time on it and then submitted it to the *Crier*.

It's colder now and there's a wind whining through the trees. Devil's Thumb looks dark and angry, almost like a warning. Shane starts the engine and gets the heater blowing. He's thinking about going home and crawling in bed with her. For all her sloppy ways, she can be sweet and she smells good, qualities he tends to forget sometimes.

Dixie closes the book and wipes her eyes with her hand. McCrae will recover and he and Harriet will get that ranch.

Redheart doesn't write it all down; it's just understood. She wishes sometimes that he would keep on going even after the story has run out, putting down the ordinary things. She feels as if there is something he isn't telling, some secret that might come out if he kept on.

"Is that book sad, is that why you're crying?" Frankie Delaney is sitting on the steps of his trailer, scratching Jewel behind the ears. It used to bother Dixie, the way he'd come out to watch her, but now she's used to him. He got hit in the head skiing when he was nine years old and his mind never grew after that. He's like a little boy in a man's body. He reminds her of her half brother Lee when he was little and used to get confused and call her Mommy.

"Did you get off for Easter?" she asks him.

"I worked this morning. I saw you come in for the doughnuts. Easter don't matter to me." He buries his face in Jewel's fur. Frankie's parents moved away from Priest Creek a year or two ago and left him here to work at the Safeway. You'd think they'd at least send him a bus ticket sometime so he could visit them. They moved to Connecticut or Vermont, she can't remember which.

She drags the cushion inside and turns it on end so she can wipe off the dirt. The place looks forlorn, dishes dirty in the sink, bed all apart. A corner of the *Shane* poster has come unstuck and is curling toward the middle. Her bra and Shane's socks are tangled on the floor.

She could clean it all up, do the dishes, even take a load to the Coin-Op. There's time to go to the Safeway and get some food, make a pan of macaroni and cheese. Louis didn't like it—all crusty on top and creamy inside—because it was too rich. He's more into brown rice and steamed vegetables, but Shane loves her macaroni and cheese. She could make that and they could eat in front of the TV, drink some cold beers, and afterward get in between some clean sheets.

She puts a Doors tape into her headset and tears the sheets off the bed, piles dirty laundry into them, ties them in a bundle, and tosses it into her car.

"Hey, Frankie, do you have any laundry? I'll give you a lift to the Coin-Op."

He jumps up, spilling Jewel onto the ground, and runs into his trailer. Dixie smiles to see him coming out with just a few things in a pillowcase. He didn't really have much laundry, just wants her company.

They're in luck because no one's there. Frankie takes care of his bundle while Dixie separates her wash into whites, lights, and darks. She buys some bleach from the vending machine and gets three machines going. It's a good sound, three machines filling up with water. Frankie's sitting in the molded plastic chair in front of his machine. "I have a red shirt in there. I like to see when it comes up," he explains.

Dixie sits beside him and watches for the red shirt to wiggle up from the rest of the clothes and press against the glass. It stays there for a while and then tunnels down to the back, or something whisks it over the top. After a time she begins to yawn, so she goes outside for a breath of air. She recognizes Dusty's pickup and Jim Cosby's parked at the Lost Dollar next door. She goes back and calls, "Frankie?"

He turns reluctantly from the machine to look at her.

"Would you tell me when my wash needs to go in the dryer?"

"Well, where're you going to be?"

"I'm just going over to the Lost Dollar to see someone. Stick your head in when the wash stops, will you?"

It looks as if all the men of Priest Creek are packed into the Lost Dollar. The ones who have families and have been with them all day because of the holiday have come to get away from them, and the ones who don't have families have come because it's lonely being without family on a holiday.

Dixie likes being in a room full of men, as long as she knows them. Something about the male bodies—it charges up the air. And they're friendlier in a group. Dusty comes over and gives her a beery kiss. Jim Cosby buys her a draft.

"Where's Shane? Didn't he come with you?" Jim looks at the door. Dixie looks too.

"I don't know where he went. I figured he'd be here. You haven't seen him?"

"I just got here. Maybe he left before I came."

"He probably has a woman someplace."

"Why would he have a woman when he has you?" Jim puts his arm around her shoulders. He has three little kids and a skinny wife who wraps meat at the Safeway.

"I don't know, it seems like he's always leaving and never tells me where he's going."

"Well, Shane, he's a complicated man."

"I know."

"He's moody."

Jim finds two stools for them at the bar. Dixie gets so interested in their talk that when Frankie comes in to tell her the wash is ready for the dryer, it seems only five minutes have passed.

"I'll be right there, soon's I finish this beer," she says. Jim has bought her another and is telling her that she might be able to work over at Eden Glen as a cook on one of the trips. "Shane was just being—you know how he gets."

"Ever since I came back from Louis's—"

"What made you go there in the first place? Louis has those glassy eyes and he doesn't talk to anybody he doesn't have to. He's not your type at all. Shane's twice the man he is. No wonder he's sore at you, d'you know what I'm saying?"

"I made it up to him. I covered the cushion in the dinette.

I'm doing his wash right now and I'm going to cook him dinner if he comes home."

"Well, that's nice. He should forgive you, if you do nice things like that for him." Jim snakes his arm down so his hand is on her breast.

She scoots out from under his arm. She has to go, her wash is ready.

"Hold on. You haven't finished your beer. Here, let me buy you some beer nuts. You like beer nuts?"

Dixie is talking to Dusty and she can't think for a moment what Frankie is doing, standing there with his pillowcase over his shoulder. Then she remembers.

"Oh my God! The wash!"

"It's too late. It's locked. It closes at seven on Sundays, Dixie."

"Why didn't you tell me?"

"I tried to and you got mad, remember? You told me to quit pestering. I just came in now because Mr. Petrillo is going to give me a ride home and he said I should tell you."

When Frankie leaves, Dixie sees that it's pitch-dark outside. Where did the afternoon go?

"Dix?"

Jewel comes out of the bedroom wagging her tail, scraping her bottom along the floor. The cushion Dixie took outside in the morning is standing on end, caked with mud. There's an empty doughnut box on the counter and the milk she bought this morning. Shane puts it in the refrigerator and takes out a piece of pizza. He bites into it, then spits it into the sink. It's green on the bottom.

The mattress is bare, the quilt is on the couch. Jewel keeps following him, whimpering. He goes to kick her, but it's not her fault. He finds some kibble in the cupboard to give her. No food for him, but there's food for her dog.

Frankie Delaney is standing by Shane's truck looking as if he had something to tell him.

"Frankie, you seen her?" Shane says.

Frankie ducks his head. He's hard to understand because he's talking into his jacket. "We went over to the Coin-Op, and while the clothes was working she went into the Lost Dollar. I told her the clothes was ready but she didn't come out. Mr. Petrillo gave me a ride home, but I don't know what she's going to do because the Coin-Op's closed now. It closes at seven on Sundays."

Anger streams through Shane, making him righteous and strong. Making him gleeful. He could laugh but he doesn't, because Frankie is watching. Instead, he clenches his jaw and leaps into his truck.

"Are you going to hit her, Shane?" Frankie throws his arms across his face as if he's seen something terrible, but it's only the headlights sweeping by.

Was it a full moon or what last night, because if it was a full moon that might explain it. Dixie can't remember any moon at all, only the headlights from Shane's truck when he cut her off as she was driving away from the Lost Dollar. Then there was the light in the open door of the Lost Dollar when everyone came out to see what was happening.

Jim Cosby and Dusty held Shane while he ranted and swore, all because of some wash left overnight. She can't recall what she said, only the feeling of choosing her fight and standing her ground, like someone from a Redheart novel when he's run all he can and now it's time to shoot it out.

All the way home she was shouting things like "I have a right, after all!" and "Why should I spend two minutes in his stinking trailer?" and "It's my life." She pulled her clothes out of the drawer and her suitcase from under the bed. And then the light bulb blew out. She went into the living room to take the bulb out of the lamp and saw the quilt, which she wrapped around herself because she was cold. She went into the bedroom with the light bulb and suddenly felt very tired, so she put her suitcase on the floor and lay down on the bed, still wrapped in the quilt. Sometime in the night, she woke up to find Shane undressing her. And then they were doing it as if it were something they'd been wanting to do all day and hadn't gotten around to. Now he's sleeping in the quilt and she's shivering on the bare mattress.

She pulls at the quilt. He grumbles but gives it up and throws an arm across her. Dixie feels his body warm against hers and remembers that making love felt good last night. But so did telling him off. But so did taking the clothes to the Coin-Op and putting them in the machines. She wishes someone would unroll the chart of her life developing so she could see the stages. Maybe she's going through one of those steps that looks wrong but later turns out to be right, like when the unborn baby grows a tail that becomes a spine later on.

Then she sits up and sees her suitcase and her clothes all over the floor and Shane's jeans crumpled on top of his boots where he left them at the side of the bed and she thinks of three machines full of wet laundry that someone will take out and pile somewhere so it will fall on the floor and get dirty all over again and she knows this can't be right. If there's a definite plan before you're born, all those steps toward getting you into your life, there must be a plan for once you're in it, and something is blocking her plan. She's like an ant that's trying to get someplace and someone keeps sticking his big old thumb in her way, making her go in crazy zigzags instead of one straight line. She gets out of bed and hugs her naked body in the cold. A life should go toward something, like it does in Treat Redheart's books. It should go forward.

CHAPTER 8

■ ■ ■

Grave Hill

They say dead men tell no tales, but take a walk sometime among the tombstones on Grave Hill. There are plenty of stories in those old inscriptions if you know how to read them.

—from the Priest Creek *Crier*

DUSTY IS LAID OUT on his couch like an effigy of a medieval knight on his tomb, his arms folded across his breast, his dog at his feet. He stretched out here just for a minute in order to open his mind, make it fertile, receptive, to allow the hard dry facts he's been amassing to brew themselves into a bubbling, frothing ferment. That was an hour and a half ago. Somehow his mental exercise turned into a common household nap. The day is nearly over, the one he dedicated to Marietta's project. She's due back from Fiji soon and she wants her legend.

She caught up with him at Lily's Easter party and accused him of avoiding her, claimed that she'd seen his back disappearing around corners all over town, told him she had to speak with him. So Dusty went up to Chez Marietta the next day, Easter Sunday. Although it was unseasonably warm, Marietta was wearing a skirt that seemed to be made out of an Indian blanket, or two of them, in yellow, green, and red. Dusty told her she looked festive. She asked if he'd brought the legend; it had been a year and she'd yet to see even a paragraph. It wasn't as if she'd asked for a piece of copy, something to go into a promotional brochure, Dusty reminded her. She had charged him with creating a love story that would endow Priest Creek with the Romance of the Old West. You can't just invent something like that. You have to research, comb through old records until the story emerges. And then you can't just write it up and impose it on a town. You have to feed it, bit by bit, into the collective unconscious, so it becomes one with the landscape, so when people drive past Bibleback Ridge or Devil's Thumb or Conners Creek, the legend comes to mind. The legend must live. It's a living thing, like bread dough, did she see?

No.

He had brought his clippings along from the Priest Creek *Crier*, the seeds of the legend. He showed her how he had been constructing the story of Bibleback Burton out of actual historical fact and writing it up for the *Crier*. He'd been planting the seeds so the legend would develop out of the matrix of Priest Creek. Marietta's forehead creased as she read the clippings. There was no story, she said, only hints about this Bibleback character—who was he, anyway?—and nothing about love. She said if Dusty didn't have the story by the time she came back from Fiji, she was going to give the job to a PR firm in Denver. He did manage to get a five-thousand-dollar advance from her, however.

So except for baking four loaves of honey-wheat bread and taking a long gestating nap, Dusty's done nothing all day but sift through old photographs, records, and newspaper clippings. The only photo he has of Bibleback Burton—and probably the only one Bibleback ever posed for—is a group shot, taken on the courthouse steps, of the sheepherders of the Ute Valley, 1885. He's almost hidden in the middle, his head tipped to one side, small, fragile-looking, but there's an intensity to those eyes, something you see in pictures of Rasputin, a burning will that can carry the soul beyond death, across a century. Lately, when Dusty's been writing a piece on the history of Priest Creek for the *Crier*, a cryptic sentence about Bibleback Burton will appear on the paper. Dusty looks at it, thinks of crossing it out, but doesn't. Bibleback is gaining a public. People are asking about him, eager for the next installment. Besides the picture, all Dusty has about Bibleback is a bill of sale for a mule he bought in '87 and a newspaper clipping on the Conners Creek lynchings—Bibleback's brother, Ethan, was one of the men who were run out of town by the marshal afterward. That's all. Not much of a story—certainly not much of a love story. Dusty should find another hero, but his hero found him, not the other way around. It isn't easy to get rid of a character once he's infiltrated the imagination.

Dusty puts his papers in order. Still in the typewriter, where he left it before stretching out for his mind experiment, is a blurb he wrote on Grave Hill for the *Crier*. Seeing it now, Dusty feels as if he's reading a message from an unseen hand. Of course. Go find Bibleback's stone in the cemetery. Afterward he can stop in at Lily's and see how Dixie's managing, take her a loaf of bread so she won't think he's spying on her. Dixie's been looking after the ranch in the month that Lily's been away.

Shortly after her guest from New York left, Lily called Dusty to tell him she was leaving. It was early in the morning. Dusty had just come in from mucking out the stable. He hadn't even had coffee yet. She was speaking a little too fast and a little too loud. It's the voice she uses when she's keeping the lid on. "I have to get away. You know, mud season. The lambs are born. There isn't much to do here but sit and worry if the creek will take the bridge out. I'm going to visit my mother for a few days . . . No, she's fine, or as well as she's going to be. I'll just check in on her and go to Saba . . . I have an old school friend there who's teaching scuba diving. I'll do some diving and help her out a little."

He offered to move into her place while she was gone and keep an eye on the livestock. She said she'd invited Dixie to stay and look after things. Dixie! She couldn't be serious. He wouldn't entrust a cat to her. But Lily's got this solidarity thing about women, that all they need is a hand up from another woman to make them strong, self-sufficient, blah blah blah. It seemed Dixie'd had a falling out with Shane. She'd been staying at Lily's learning what there was to do. She was looking forward to being on her own and running the place. It would be good for both of them. Dusty promised he'd look in on Dixie from time to time. There was an unspoken understanding between them that, for all her good intentions, Dixie was capable of messing things up royally and would bear watching.

Dusty can't remember Lily ever going away for mud season, although most of the people in Priest Creek who can afford it do so. Lily didn't say, but Dusty knows it's the stranger from New York—the one who came to ski and never made it to the slopes—who forced her out of her home. He left his hairs on her pillow, his pheromones soaked into the wood of her hot tub. It is his tormenting absence that is keeping her away so long.

Dusty should have gone with her. He almost said he would, until he remembered that his credit lines had run out, his cards were defunct, and the five thousand Marietta had advanced him had already disappeared into the black hole of debt. It's not that Dusty's expenses are so great; it's just that his income is so meager—a cash-flow problem.

At the Post Office there's a card from Lily with a picture

of a parrot fish and some coral. "I'm discovering a whole world. I'm growing gills . . . paradise . . . the colors." Dusty worries that she'll get rapture of the deep and forget to surface.

As Dusty's pickup splashes through puddles and shudders over washouts on Conners Creek Road, he imagines Lily swimming ten fathoms deep. Silver bubbles stream behind her, tangling in her silver hair. Flippered feet send her gliding through schools of bright, dappled fish. Soft tentacles undulate in her wake. Dusty drinks from a can of Moosehead beer he keeps in a holder on the dashboard. Mile-high clouds rolling like giant sponges along the horizon are mirrored in flooded pasture so that the cattle seem suspended among them. Under these clouds, sunlight streams in horizontally, picking out the stones on Grave Hill, making them gleam preternaturally white. Dusty feels a glow in his chest and the certainty that there is a message for him there, the key to a story that will link past to present, woman to man, that will bring Dusty something even more precious than the next five thousand Marietta promised him, although that too will be useful.

He turns into Lily's drive. Conners Creek is spilling its banks, but the bridge looks solid. Dixie must be still at work over at Louis's upholstery. The door isn't locked, but Lily never locks it either. There are dirty dishes in the sink but nothing terrible. The bed's unmade; Dixie's using Lily's bed. There's a pair of lace underpants on the floor and a bra (C cup), flannel shirt, jeans, a dirty glass by the bed (milk), and a book, *The Gentle Warrior*, one of those mystical self-help books. There's a whole section of the bookstore in town devoted to such works. A struggle has been going on here. Dixie has been wrestling with her own nature, trying to find the stairway to higher consciousness. The lace drawers are silky and good quality. They remind him that one can never know everything about a person.

He hears a horn—Dixie coming up through the cotton-woods, warning the mouflons out of the way. He stuffs the pants into his pocket and hurries downstairs. He's leaning casually against the counter, drinking a beer, when she comes in. "I thought I'd come by and see how you were getting on," he says.

"Oh good. You can help me get Simone back up the hill. She keeps jumping the fence and messing around by the creek. She's worse than the mule. Lily's spoiled her something terrible." Dixie's pulled her hair back at the nape of her neck and fastened it with a barrette, which makes her look more adult and also demure. Her flannel shirt is tucked into her jeans, showing her full bosom and neat waist. He hands her a beer. She hesitates. "I've been on kind of a health kick since I came here, you know, eating brown rice and all. Herb teas."

"Well, don't let me be a corrupting influence."

"I guess one beer isn't going to hurt anything."

"Have you heard from the Jacques Cousteau of Priest Creek?"

"Who? Oh, Lily. Just some postcards. It sounds like she's having the neatest time. I write her long letters about the animals, you know, so she won't forget to come back."

"Has she said anything about that—coming back?"

"Uh-uh. I reckon she's just havin' herself a ball and she knows I've got everything in hand . . ."

After the beers, which Dixie says went right to her head because she's not used to drinking anymore, they decide to go out and catch that thundering Arabian before she steps in a marmot hole or something. The minute she sees them coming with the bridle, she runs. She's a beauty. Her mane looks bleached white in the dusk, reminding Dusty of silver hair flowing behind a diver. She carries her tail high and switches it saucily. By the time they corner her, Dusty is winded. Dixie is rosy and laughing. She slips the bridle on easily and the mare follows as docilely as if she'd intended to come all along, just thought she'd give them a little exercise. Dixie hoists herself on bareback. This gives Dusty an opportunity to admire their firm and rounded rumps.

Dixie rubs the horse down and gives her a brushing. Dusty forks over some hay. One of the lambs, Moosehead, named for the bottle he drinks from, is pestering Dixie. She milks the cashmere goat and fills Moosehead's bottle. "Dusty, you staying for dinner? I'm warning you, I'm cooking a new way, everything healthy and good for you, no chicken-fried steak and gravy."

Dusty says that's fine with him. He'll feed Moosehead while she sees to dinner. He sits on a bale of hay and holds the bottle out. "Come to Mama, little man." It's strange being around Lily's animals without her, because they are her thoughts incarnate. All of them, the horse, the mule, the sheep, the goat, were bred by Lily, so before they quickened in their mothers' wombs, they were generated in Lily's mind. If anyone has a window on Lily's soul, it's one of these dumb animals. He looks deep into Moosehead's eyes, as if there were answers there that he could read.

Dinner is vegetable curry, not bad. Dixie's been experimenting with a vegetarian cookbook, learning a lot about nutrition, she says. It helps to have Dusty's bread with it and a bottle of red wine that he picked up on impulse while he was filling the tank earlier at the gas station and drive-in liquor store. After dinner they drift into the living room in front of the stove. Dusty takes the chair and Dixie sprawls on the couch, one knee drawn up close, the other leg dangling. Dusty wonders if she is wearing lace pants under the jeans. "So it's really over between you and Shane, huh?" he says, not really caring, making conversation.

"Yeah, I guess. We're—you know—we're not good for each other, Dusty. Well, you saw us that night in front of the Lost Dollar. We get like that a lot, out of control. It's, you know, it's not good."

"It never seemed as if you had that much in common," Dusty says just to encourage her.

"Yeah, you know, you're right. Like, I can't remember ever having a conversation with Shane like me and you are having right now. Just a conversation." She drinks her wine. Inside the stove, a log drops with a soft hiss. "Of course, the thing is, we did have good sex. There's nothing wrong with us in that department. There's nothing wrong with us in that department, you can count on that. Even that night, after you helped break up our fight? Things were hot back in the old trailer later, you wouldn't have believed."

Dusty tells himself this would be an excellent time to leave, although it would be uncomfortable to stand right now.

"I don't know how Lily does it," Dixie says. "I mean, I can do without alcohol. I could go without meat for the rest of my life, I don't care, wouldn't miss it, but even a week without a man and I start going crazy."

In the blue light of early day, when Dusty is stealing home like a guilty thief, it occurs to him that the message in Moosehead's eyes was that Dusty was a goddamn fool. It had something to do with extreme sensitivity to initial conditions, one of Dusty's favorite phrases from Chaos Theory. It seems in a chaotic system (and anything involving Dixie involves chaos) one minor event at the beginning can tip the entire system a certain way. In this case it was finding Dixie's lace drawers. He never should have gone up to the bedroom. After those silk pants, the rest was preordained. He didn't need the chase through the field after the mare, the sight of the two rumps on the way back to the barn. He didn't need dinner, the red wine, the confession about how hard it is for her to do without sex.

"Don't tell Lily," he begged her later, like a little boy. He knows she will—part of their female bond. Lily might just as well have put a marking harness on him when she left, the way she does with the rams to see who's mounting whom.

Grave Hill flashes in his peripheral vision. He slams on the brakes, then backs up. This is what brought him out in the first place. He might as well look around to see if he can find anything useful. The grass is brown, the hair of a dead beast, with mud, like corrupting flesh oozing up through. Someone has strung barbed wire to keep livestock out and there's a sturdy gate with a sign that says this is the oldest graveyard in Ute County. Dusty remembers that this was one of Marietta's reauthenticating projects. The old tombstones, sober blocks, are up front. Some are broken. Some are sinking into the earth. Finally he finds, intact, a stone saying *Ethan Burton b. 1854 d. 1920*, and under that, with a line to separate them, *Cora Burton b. 1859 d. 1932*. There are two smaller stones for children, one d. 1884, age two years seven months and three days, and one d. 1892, age four years three months and twelve days.

And what about Bibleback? He has to be here someplace. Dusty tramps around until his boots are heavy with mud, but nothing. How could Bibleback, after having insinuated himself into practically every historical piece Dusty's written for the *Crier*, disappear now, at this critical time, when the five thousand has been taken and spent? Yesterday Dusty felt so hopeful, so close to enlightenment, on the trail of love, and suddenly it has turned cold, as cold as stone. He thrusts his hands in his pockets and feels something slippery. He fingers it absentmindedly, then remembers and groans out loud.

CHAPTER 9

■ ■ ■

Doubles Match

WHEN FOSTER FLEW OUT this morning, New York looked doomed; its towers were shrouded in yellow smog. And Denver, where he landed to get the jumper flight, was worse—a grid of flat box buildings sprawling under a brown haze. Uniform formlessness. Now, from the window of the Dash 7, he sees miles of evergreen forest with lighter islands of aspen and the dwellings of man sanely clustered at the elbow of the creek. Innocent, invisible air. He's been away too long.

If it hadn't been for Bella he wouldn't be here even now. She fell in love with Lily without meeting her, just from Foster's stories. Bella pored over the photos Foster had taken, putting together faces of the children Foster and Lily would have. But even as Bella was dreaming, the distance between Foster and Lily was increasing. Not long after Foster went back to New York, Lily took off for the Caribbean on a whim, or at least it seemed whimsical to Foster, because she never told him she was going. He called one night and another woman answered the phone, said she was looking after the place while Lily was away. It was a definite letdown. Foster had attached himself, not only to Lily, but to Lily on her ranch, Lily and her animals; then suddenly, without warning, Lily wrenched herself out of context and went to the Caribbean, of all places. After phoning a few more times and getting that woman, who couldn't or wouldn't tell him any more about why Lily had left or when she'd be back ("I reckon she'll get here when she gets here"), Foster stopped calling. Work picked up.

Bella began to mourn Lily and the grandchildren she would never have. Was it fair to demand so many grandchildren when she herself had had only one child, Foster asked her. She would have had five, she said. It was Foster's father who'd decided that one was sufficient. Bella, a career woman all the while Foster was growing up, is turning into an earth mother in her later years. She wants to visit Foster and Lily on Lily's ranch, milk goats, and tend grandchildren. Bella talked him into calling Lily again. Lily would certainly be home by now, Bella said. No one stays in the Caribbean in the summer.

It gave him a shock at first to hear Lily's voice—deep, strong, reminding him right away of who Lily is. He had planned to begin by asking why she left without telling him, put her on the defensive before she could ask why he hadn't called. It was a tactic he would have used with any other woman, but Lily's voice demanded something better. "Look, I'm sorry we drifted apart. I tried to call you but you were away, and then I got caught up in things here— I wasn't sure how you felt—could I come out and see you," he said. There was an intake of breath, or it might have been static on the line, and then she said certainly, when would he like to come? He gave her a date. She said she was playing in a tennis tournament and holding a barbecue afterward, but that was fine; he could help out. When he called back to tell her his flight, he got the answering machine. He left the information; Lily never called back.

As Foster climbs out of the plane into the brilliant daylight, he tells himself that Lily never would have said he could come if she didn't mean it. Lily is not in the terminal.

He retrieves his bag and goes outside, where Lily's white pickup is idling at the curb. He runs over, tosses his bag into the back with the straw, the sheep manure, and jumps lightly into the passenger side. He's already reached over to kiss the driver before he realizes it isn't Lily.

She grabs the back of his neck and completes the kiss with a sharp hot tongue. "I reckon that wasn't for me, but I'll take it anyway. Finders keepers. Now don't tell me you don't know who I am. Dixie," she reminds him. "The reason you don't recognize me is I lost so much weight. I'm living up at Lily's now, helping her out with the animals and helping myself too, you know—"

"Where's Lily?"

Dixie turns onto the road. "Out hiking the Colorado Trail with some llamas."

"She didn't tell me—"

"This just came up kind of last minute. She and the Turrells started this service, where the llamas carry the baggage so the hikers don't have to."

"When will she be back?"

"Tomorrow."

"Are you sure?"

"Oh yeah. She has to be back tomorrow. It's the tournament."

Lily's ranch astounds him with its beauty. He'd forgotten, or maybe he'd looked at the photos too often. A photograph diminishes. It can't capture the play of light on weathered timbers, can't convey the sounds of roosters crowing, lambs bleating. He goes to the barn prepared to see pens of ewes and newborn lambs, but the barn is empty, swept clean. Something swoops past his head like a mocking spirit. Then another. They're birds with forked tails, gliding through as if the barn didn't exist. The night of the stars and the lamb, how easily he accepted it as his due.

He left trusting that it would remain for him unchanged until he returned.

Dusty is having a beer at the Lost Dollar when Dixie walks in and takes the stool next to him. He orders her a beer. "So what happened? Did your resolutions give way before a mighty thirst? Demon rum get the better of you?" he asks.

"Lily's sweetheart from New York is visiting, so I thought I'd give them some space."

"What's he doing here? He sure took his time getting back," Dusty says.

"He's nuts about her." Dixie looks around the bar. "I thought Shane would be here."

"How long's he staying?"

"Shane? Oh, Foster. I don't know, a week—two maybe. Was he in earlier?"

"What would he come here for?"

"Shane? Oh, Foster. I don't know, Dusty. Maybe Lily asked him out to watch her play in the tournament tomorrow. I wonder where he is."

Dusty looks down the bar. "I thought you and Shane were finished. I thought that was why you were staying at Lily's in the first place, to get away from Shane." Not that Dusty cares. He's shied away from Dixie since that night at Lily's.

Dixie takes a swig of beer and licks the foam off her upper lip. "Lily doesn't really know Shane. She thinks he's a loser who drinks too much. She's got this idea that as soon as I find my center and get my self-respect I won't want Shane anymore. So if I go to bed with Shane I'm a failure. See how that works?"

Dusty decides to invest some change in the jukebox. When he comes back, Dixie says, "Lily thinks I should find someone like you, someone sensitive. She says you're—"

"You told her about me, didn't you, about you and me that time."

"Well, yeah."

"I asked you not to."

"I can't lie to Lily, Dusty."

"I bet she just dragged it out of you."

"It came out in conversation." Dixie's wearing her hair like Lily, but her shirt's unbuttoned one more than Lily would go. She pulls her stool closer to Dusty. "You know, it's real funny. I can't understand it, but somehow thinking Lily doesn't know makes it more exciting. I saw Shane in the Safeway the other day, in the produce section, and we didn't say a word. We just went through the checkout and back to his place and we—"

"You don't have to tell me this."

"It's just peculiar, you know. And then he comes into the shop when I'm there alone and he—"

"For Chrissakes."

"Standing up in the back—"

"Dixie, Dixie, listen. All you have to do is tell Lily you're going back with Shane. She'll understand."

"I can't do that. You know Lily. She gets an idea—I can't disappoint her. Besides, it's kind of exciting, you know, meeting in funny places. It's romantic."

"You're lying to Lily," he tells Dixie. "It's not fair to Lily and it's not fair to yourself in the long run, because more than anything Lily appreciates honesty. You know she's going to find out, sooner or later. When a person like Lily offers you friendship, it's an honor. You have to respect it."

"You know, Dusty, you'd make a good judge. You should be a real one. Not just judge of the tennis tournament and the Jell-O Jump."

The Jell-O Jump. Come, he tells her, let's dance this slow number. Don't trip on the linoleum where it's coming up there.

Through the skylights Dusty sees high puffy clouds alternating with clear blue. The breeze coming in the open window is not too strong. It's a perfect day for the tournament. Couldn't ask for better. He's kneading bread— olive walnut, something new—to take over to Lily's afterward. Sweat drops off his nose onto the dough. He folds it in. A little salt won't hurt, it's what gives it that homemade flavor. He's kneading vigorously, keeping time with an early Stones album.

"Jiminy Jaysus. I thought you were hammering something. You're pounding the daylights out of that." A round rosy bottom appears at the top of the ladder to his loft.

"Don't come down here like that. Put something on," he says.

"Do you have a dress code here or something? I just want to take a bath." She reappears in one of his work shirts, which fits her like a dress. In bare feet she comes up to his armpit. "Why don't you give that poor thing a rest and I'll show you something I do for Shane sometimes."

Dusty slams the dough on the board. He kneads until bubbles appear under the skin and it squeaks for mercy. The album ends. Over the sound of the bathtub filling, he hears Dixie warbling some country tune. Dusty covers the dough with a towel and wipes the bread board clean. The taps are off now and from the bathroom comes a gentle sloshing and a sweet sad song. She's tied her hair out of the way with the lace from Dusty's boot.

The water has turned cold. Dusty disentangles himself and looks at his watch. "Christ. I should be there by now." The bread. Dixie says she'll finish it, put it in the pans, let it rise, bake it for twenty-five minutes. Of course she knows how to bake bread. She'll see him there. Dusty is relacing his boot, not looking at her. "Don't tell Lily about this, okay?"

She steps out of the tub and wraps a towel around herself. "What is this about Lily? I feel like one of her ewes she's decided not to let mate this year. Whenever I want it I have to go hide in the bushes."

The tennis courts are in Ski Town, behind the Sheraton at the bottom of the hill where you ski out at the end of the day, Lily told him. Foster reminded her that he never did go skiing that week.

This isn't a tennis crowd. It's the group that comes out for everything in Priest Creek, from high-school football to rodeos. The spectators have spread blankets on the hill, brought sandwiches and beers, kids and dogs, are making a day of it. The announcer sitting on a crate, a bearded guy with a Day-Glo cap, someone who looks familiar to Foster, does not have a firm grasp of tennis terms and doesn't pretend to. Although the players are good, there is a casualness, a feeling that this is only one more thing they do together to have a good time. That competitive edge you'd find in the East at something like this is not present. When Foster described Priest Creek to Bella, he told her that it was where people with Type B personalities go to live and laugh at the Type A's sweating it out in the cities. And so with this match, there's a light mockery of the strict conventions of the East.

Lily, however, in her tennis dress and visor could easily pass at Forest Hills. Foster was taken aback when she appeared in her getup. It looked incongruous, those bale-pitching arms coming out of the Forest Hills dress, and it bothered him, the same way her going to the Caribbean had. It took her out of context.

Lily left him here, stranded on a corner of a handwoven, all-natural, undyed wool blanket with the sheep people. She didn't bother introducing him because he'd met them last time he was here—a couple and their small son, all wearing T-shirts that say *I'm feeling sheepish*. The only problem was that Foster couldn't remember their names. Finally, some people came over and called them Chris and Irene.

"It's my fault Lily wasn't here yesterday when you got in," Irene tells Foster. "Some lambs were sick and I didn't want to be left alone with them, so I asked Lily to take Chris's place on the hike. She said, 'Sure, no problem,' never mentioned that you were coming in. You know Lily."

No, he doesn't, Foster realizes. He doesn't know Lily, not well.

"I love watching those two play." Irene is talking about Lily and her doubles partner, the way they know where the other one is, the parity and respect between them. Everything that went wrong between Foster and his wife is going right with Lily and her partner. What was his name? He looks familiar. "Ad in," the announcer is saying. "If they make this it's game set match and it's all over. But don't pack up your beer and babies yet. Let's watch Lily do her thing."

Lily arches back, then snaps her body forward. The ball skids into the corner, just inside the line. Her partner sweeps her into a hug and her feet leave the ground. Foster jumps up and loses sight of Lily. There's Dixie, the announcer, a lot of people Foster's never seen before. Then the crowd opens. Lily is tucked under her partner's arm, as if he won her. A pretty blonde hands them both beers and gives the man a kiss. "Is that blonde his wife?" Foster asks Irene.

Irene picks up the blanket. "They just got married. Nadine. She's real nice."

"And the announcer's a friend of Lily's?"

"You met him at Lily's party, didn't you? You must have. Dusty goes to all Lily's things."

"Dusty, that's right." Is he sleeping with her? is what Foster wants to ask. He wants to ask that about all the men gathered around Lily.

Chris has already started out with his little boy. "We'll see you at the barbecue," Irene says.

Foster is alone now in a crowd where everyone knows everyone else. He feels as if he's becoming invisible, losing power. He's too far from his transmitting station, his source—too far from work, Bella, even his wife. They beam power to him. But here he is on unfamiliar terrain. This is Lily's land and he's only a stranger passing through.

"What future could there be for Lily and me?" he asked Bella. "I can't live on a ranch in Colorado and make commercials. She can't live in Brooklyn and raise sheep." Bella said that Foster could think of something. He could write his music in Colorado and come to New York to record. He could take Nicholas for summers. Life out West might be the child's salvation. Bella says the city is falling apart —the homeless in the street, like downtown Calcutta; children selling crack, getting shot through their bedroom walls. It's time to flee to the mountains, where she's never been. He tries to imagine Bella visiting Lily, wearing one of her suits, her commodious bag tucked under her arm, picking her way in heels through the mud to the barn, or, as bad, wearing new boots purchased for the occasion.

Suddenly Lily is beside him. "Let's get out of here. We still have to set up for the party," she says.

He circles her with his arm, pulls her toward him. "You were fantastic," he says.

Lily traditionally throws a barbecue after the tennis tournament. It comes at a good time, the weekend after the county fair. The 4-H lambs, the ones Lily sold to the children to raise, have been judged and slaughtered, and Lily buys one back to roast whole on a spit over an open fire. Everyone brings something: salad, beer, wine, a casserole. Dusty hooks up speakers in the yard and makes sure there's music all the time. The guests are old friends, the people she relies on and who rely on her to help get the hay in, to find a lost lamb, to plow a driveway. The only one here who doesn't fit into the web of shared responsibilities is Foster.

"Don't these look fantastic, Lily?" Dixie puts three dark loaves on the picnic table. "They have black olives and walnuts in them. I don't know how Dusty comes up with his ideas. I finished baking them because he had to leave, to do the announcing, you know." Dixie arranges them, her trophies from a night spent with Dusty. When Lily returned from Saba, Dixie was eager to let her know that she and Dusty had slept together in Lily's own bed. Lily had assumed she was joking, which hurt Dixie's feelings —didn't Lily think Dixie was good enough for Dusty? Lily said she'd just never thought of Dixie and Dusty together. The truth was, she told Dixie, she never thought of Dusty with any woman: he seemed celibate, monkish in his little cabin by the creek. Dixie laughed too long and too hard, and said that Dusty was known as the "dirty old man" of Priest Creek, etc. Although Lily never said anything, she'd felt left out and even—absurdly—betrayed. Now, watching Dixie caressing the loaves with a proprietary hand, Lily feels a constriction in her chest. It's childish of her, petty. She tells herself that Dusty would be a better choice for Dixie than Shane.

She looks at Dusty talking to Buzzy, holding a beer in one hand and absentmindedly caressing his belly with the other. Dixie, following the direction of Lily's gaze, saunters over. Buzzy gives her a perfunctory nod, but Dusty doesn't give her even that much. She could be a cat passing through the grass. Maybe Dusty's very indifference is an indication that there is something between them.

Human mating practices have always been mysterious to Lily. They're not confined to any season or age, and they are so intermingled with other motives that it's hard to tell if the driving force is sex or something else. Foster, passing with more beers to put in the cooler, gives Lily an affectionate squeeze. Is it because he likes her—a gesture of sexual attraction—or is he signaling to the other males that she is his territory?

When Foster called and asked if he could come, Lily regretted saying yes as soon as she hung up the phone. She thought of calling back and telling him not to, but kept putting it off. Then Irene asked her to take Chris's place on the hike and she accepted. This way she didn't have to meet Foster at the airport and be alone with him the first night. It was easier to rush home, play in the tournament, get the barbecue together. It's given her time to absorb his presence—a quick glance at his face, the press of his hand, taking him in slow sips, getting used to him again, bracing herself for the way he's going to scramble up her life.

Dusty is carving the lamb. He stops to take a plate to Lily, turning his back once more on Dixie. Dixie doesn't seem to mind. She has her neighbor, Frankie Delaney, in tow. She helps him fix a plate.

Dusty comes over with a plate for Lily. "This part's pink; I saved it for you because you like it rare."

Foster tenders some lettuce on a fork. "Lily, taste the salad. Is there too much vinegar for you?" She lifts the lettuce off with her fingers. "Perfect," she says, but she can't meet his eyes.

"Lily, did you try my bread?" Dusty hands her a slice.

"Mmm. Different. Kind of peculiar, but I like it. Great with lamb." She rests her eyes on her old friend's face, deliberately holding it a little longer than necessary, as an experiment. She can't meet Foster's eyes, but she could look forever into Dusty's. It's Dusty who looks away first.

Something Foster said last time he visited comes back to her, about how she controls everything on her ranch: life, death, reproduction. She holds the power. Even when Jerry was alive, she couldn't control his drugs or his drinking, but she could predict it. He couldn't surprise her, and after the first few times, he couldn't hurt her.

Her friends are lining up, filling their plates, talking, joking. Does anyone suspect how he frightens her, this man who is standing with his arm protectively around her shoulder, this stranger who's come to town?

CHAPTER 10

■ ■ ■

Sulfur Cave

Sulfur Cave, wrapped in legend and steeped in toxic fumes, is located on the west side of Outlaw Hill, close to the summit. Those who enter never return.

—from the Priest Creek *Crier*

DUSTY IS in the Sunrise Café, at his usual table with a view of Main and Hoyt Streets, polishing up a background piece on the high-school football team for the *Crier* while waiting for his breakfast. Joyce sets his eggs before him and he drowns them in pepper. He's just tucking in when a shadow falls across his plate. Marietta! He jumps up, an escape move, but manages to convert it into a gentlemanly gesture. He invites her to take the chair opposite him. When did she get back in town? Last night, she says. She is wearing an elaborate cowrie-shell neckpiece but doesn't want to talk about why she returned from Fiji so abruptly. She had extended her original stay for so long that Dusty had begun to think that he'd never have to deliver on the five thousand she'd advanced him. Rumors had her involved in a real-estate deal there, or in a love affair with a local. Both may have been true.

Beneath her tan, Marietta looks sallow. Crow's-feet have crept into the corners of her eyes. She's lost her sense of humor. He is trying to explain that although he doesn't have the actual manuscript to give her, the hard part is over. The legend is there; all the pieces are falling into place. The only thing left is to write it up. His fingers flutter over his congealing eggs as if the typewriter were superimposed upon them, the carriage flying as he turns out the story. Why the hell did he ever take the five thousand? He's been too ready to take whatever's come his way— Dixie, the five thousand. He should have turned down Marietta. He pictures himself pushing money away (stacked in neat bundles) and Marietta dissolving into dots.

But she is very much there, blocking his view of Main Street, playing halfheartedly with a piece of cantaloupe and a cup of black coffee, the distillation of disappointment. It must have more to do with Fiji than with him, but he's bearing the brunt. Come, he says, we'll take my truck. When you see this—you have to see it; I won't spoil it by telling you first—but it's the proof, the keystone. Her boots are custom-made cowboy packers, designed for rough wear, but they look as if they've never been off pavement. No matter. It hasn't rained in weeks. The mud will be dry by now.

She brightens when she sees they're heading for Grave Hill. "I had that historical marker put there. It's the oldest graveyard in the valley. It beats the one in Telluride by seven years."

Dusty takes her elbow to lead her to the Burton family plot. He squats next to the smallest tombstone, one with a lamb chiseled into it. *Rebekah Burton d. 1892, age four years three months and twelve days.*

"I think those little graves are the saddest things." Marietta wipes her eyes.

She doesn't get it. Dusty didn't either when he first saw it. He had to go back and look a second time. Rebekah was born in 1888, two years after Ethan Burton was run out of town for lynching Conner. She was Bibleback's child. Why Bibleback's, she asks. Why not someone else's? Think of the times, he urges her—a hundred years ago—a man has to leave town. He puts someone in charge of his family—his deformed brother.

"Then where's Bibleback? Bibleback isn't here."

"Ethan came back, see—"

"And Bibleback ran off?"

"Well, that's a possibility, but I'm afraid it was worse than that." Dusty looks at the little grave. "I'm afraid Bibleback took his own life."

"Then his grave would be here, or somewhere. There'd be a death certificate. You've gone through the records, haven't you? At least you've done that." Fiji was definitely not good for her.

Sulfur Cave, Dusty tells her. Up Outlaw Hill. Bibleback rides his mule up there one day and never comes back. Ethan finds the mule later, still saddled, covered with mud, grazing beside the other livestock.

"I love it! And if it's true, the skeleton will be in the cave."

"Never found. No one can go in there. The fumes."

"Not then, but today. With a tank and a mask, one of those moon suits. We just have to find someone who does that kind of thing, a toxic-waste person, and send him or her in to look for the skeleton. And it will be deformed. Oh neat! That's how we'll know." Marietta's color is coming back. Her eyes are dancing.

"Marietta, it's ghoulish to want his bones. It's enough, isn't it, to have his story, to have an idea of the way it went. We don't need his actual misshapen vertebrae in our—"

"We have to *know*. I don't want illusion. I want fact."

Marietta's chins wobble. The ravens jeer. Aspens at the edge of the graveyard shake their leaves in silent, heartless mirth. He never should have taken the five thousand.

When Dusty drops Marietta off at the Sunrise, he is surprised to see Lily's white truck at the curb. Her visits to town always have a purpose: there's a Town Council meeting, a 4-H thing, or she has a tennis match. She doesn't come in for a cup of coffee and a casual chat. But she is there, at Dusty's table in the window, and she is alone. Must just have taken New York to the airport.

Lily waves to Dusty. She was hoping he'd come back; Joyce said he might. He asks Joyce for two eggs over easy and sits opposite Lily, scanning her face as if he expects to find something new.

"We sure could use some rain," Lily says.

"It's dry as tinder. The Forest Service has banned campfires," Dusty says.

"So I heard."

"We've got one of those high-pressure systems sitting over us. The longer it stays, the drier it gets. It's a self-perpetuating kind of thing."

"Is that right?" Lily stirs her coffee. "I haven't seen Dixie in a while," she says. "Is she staying over with you now?"

Dusty's face hardens. "Why would she be staying with me?"

"I understood the two of you had something going—"

Dusty bends over his plate. Lily feels as if there's a high-pressure system over their table, impeding the flow of conversation, making it dry and brittle. She'd been hoping to talk to Dusty about Foster. She has plenty of friends in Priest Creek, but her conversations with them are all about practical matters. For personal matters, there are only two people Lily would consider talking to: Dixie and Dusty.

Dixie is good in that she'll talk about anything, but Lily doesn't trust her judgment. That leaves Dusty.

"Lily, I—" Dusty startles her by taking her hand across the table. His palm is broad and meaty, his fingers short, so different from Foster's slender, pliable hand. Joyce comes to take Dusty's plate and pour more coffee. "No thanks." Dusty waves her away. "We have to get moving if we're going to ride up Outlaw Hill and get back by dark."

"You're riding up there?" Lily asks.

"You and me, if you'll come, that is. One and Two need the exercise."

Dusty pays and shepherds Lily out the door. She goes along, mainly because she doesn't feel up to facing her empty house.

Dusty is riding Horse II and Lily is following on Horse I.

"You named these mares wrong, Dusty. One always wants to go behind Two."

"I named One One because I got her first. It's just another instance of their ornery natures that they travel this way."

They talk about the mares, how they've been spoiled by poor riders at the Eden Glen Guest Ranch; they talk about how they could sure use some rain. What they don't talk about, and Dusty can feel how badly Lily wants to, is Foster. But it would be better if they didn't, because Dusty hasn't felt such instinctive dislike toward another human being since Jerry was alive. It worries him to think that Lily might make another disastrous match, but what can he say to Lily—what can he do? He isn't, after all, Lily's keeper.

So Dusty begins telling Lily about Bibleback, someone who lived a hundred years ago, someone who's nothing to either one of them. "He was a scrawny little guy, short,

because of his hump. I have a picture of him back at the
house, one of those group shots where they lined everyone
up. He's just a face, but it will give you an idea of his size."
　Bibleback didn't make excuses for himself. He was feisty.
Homesteaded a ranch. It didn't work out, but that wasn't
his fault. He was too poor and misshapen to attract a wife.
Too proud to pay for one of the whores who lived on
Paradise Road. He was a virgin. When his ranch failed, his
brother, Ethan, invited him to move in with him, his wife,
Cora, and his two young sons. Ethan knew Bibleback was
a worker, and Ethan could use an extra hand, so it wasn't
just charity. "Bibleback was the older brother, did I mention that?"
　He turns to Lily riding behind him. She's thinking of
lover boy, but Dusty wants her to concentrate on what
torture it was for Bibleback, living in the same small cabin
with Ethan and Cora. She knows what those small cabins
were like—walls so thin they might as well not have been
there. In the winter there would be female undergarments
drying by the stove. Bibleback would catch her scent every
time she came near. He'd brush against her, often touch
her, and they'd both pretend it wasn't happening.
　Bibleback had been living with his brother for over a
year. He woke up earlier than usual one morning (he slept
in the loft with his nephews). Down below he could hear
his brother with Cora, and Bibleback reached for himself
so he could accompany their rhythmical rocking with his
own lonely instrument. They came to conclusion in a cho-
rus of sighs, more or less at the same time. Bibleback lay
there, curled around himself, and then, before anyone else
was up, he stole down the ladder, threw together some
cornmeal, a slab of salt pork, enough to keep himself alive
for three days, tied his bedroll on the back of his saddle,
and rode off on his mule. His plan was to keep traveling,
finding work as he went. He got as far as Devil's Thumb.

There's a spring at the base of it—does Lily know where he means?

The horses have stopped to suck up water from a stream. Lily says she knows the spring, but how does Dusty know all this about Bibleback? He's making it up, isn't he? Dusty says he knows the essential facts. They are a matter of public record. He is only filling in the details. Lily says there seem to be a lot of details. Dusty is delighted he's caught her interest. He'll go all day inventing details if it will keep her from talking about Foster. Two has been sneaking grass from the side of the stream. Dusty jerks her head up and they continue.

Bibleback intended to stretch his legs, have his lunch, and let the mule graze a bit before continuing his journey, but he became very sleepy and decided to take a nap while the sun was high. He slept longer than he'd planned. When he woke, although there were many hours of daylight left, it didn't seem worthwhile to move on that day. He made camp. The next morning he got up, had some coffee, and saddled the mule. But he couldn't bring himself to get on. After a while he took the saddle off and let the mule out to graze. He stayed by the Devil's Thumb all day, watching its colors change from gold to copper to lead in the moonlight. The third day, Bibleback rode home. He felt calmer, as if something had been resolved, although he couldn't say what.

Then, in the early fall, round about this time as a matter of fact, Bibleback found what he had been looking for but hadn't known it—an elk carcass, a fresh kill, shot through the heart, the head removed and the hide. The meat had been left to rot. Bibleback brought Ethan to see the carcass. Ethan went wild. They searched all day and around dusk came upon the camp by Conners Creek—

"This is the lynching story, the one you wrote up for the paper," Lily says, proving he has her attention.

She knows this part, but what she doesn't know is that Bibleback spoke to Conner first and was so arrogant and menacing that Conner lost his temper and ran him out of camp with his shotgun. Then Bibleback manipulated his brother into putting together a lynching party. Bibleback went along but stayed in the back and let Ethan take charge.

The marshal sympathized with the homesteaders, but he couldn't let a lynching go unpunished. He ordered the leaders—Ethan and another man—to leave town. Bibleback was allowed to stay so that he could take care of Ethan's family and property. The townspeople and Ethan (and possibly Cora) regarded Bibleback as a kind of eunuch because of his small size and his hump, so no one had a problem about this man and woman living together. Bibleback, however, now that he was living with Cora without Ethan around, turned out to have very winning ways. Perhaps because his deformity had forced him to be an outsider, an observer, Bibleback was more attuned to other people's emotions than most men of his time. Bibleback began performing little acts of kindness for Cora, unobtrusively helping her when she had to perform heavy chores. He even sewed together a scarf out of rabbit fur and gave it to her for Christmas.

"Did she fall in love with him?" Lily asks.

"She had his child."

"Really?"

" 'Course, that made people suspicious."

"It would."

"Word got around to Ethan, who hadn't gone that far away, just up to Laramie, and he came home."

"And she let him?"

"What could she do? She was his legal wife, living on his land. So Bibleback kissed his baby daughter goodbye, and got on his mule. He intended to move on somewhere, find work, but his mule headed up Outlaw Hill, and when Bibleback saw Sulfur Cave, he got off and walked into the cave."

They ride in silence for a while, until the horses snort and shake their heads.

"They must have caught a whiff of the sulfur," Dusty says. "Let's lead them around until they're upwind."

They tether One and Two well away from the cave and go the rest of the way on foot. Someone has erected a barricade across the entrance with a skull-and-crossbones sign. The barricade is flimsy, but it would take a desperate person to break through it and enter this crack in the earth, this brown crusted wound. Dusty shines a flashlight in; Lily sees a glint of yellow crystals. Out here, the fumes tickle the throat and nose. Inside, it would burn and choke. Would you keep walking in, deeper and deeper, even though your eyes were blinded, your guts twisting?

"I hope he's in there," Dusty says.

"What?"

"His bones. I hope they're in there."

"So this isn't certain?"

"Nothing is certain."

"Well, I hope he isn't. I hope he rode off and found a new woman and made a new life for himself."

"That wouldn't be a story. It would be an incident, nothing more. He has to be in there."

"You make it sound like he owes it to you, this poor cripple. What's it to you if he killed himself for love or not? So long ago."

They have lunch back where the horses are tied, away from the sulfur fumes—leftover cold chicken and Dusty's homemade sourdough bread. The wind is fresh, with just a hint of chill to it. Dusty feels an enormous relief that has partly to do with knowing that Foster has left and partly with finally getting the story of Bibleback out, getting it told. Now it exists. And Lily likes Bibleback. She doesn't want his bones to be in the cave.

"So what's up with you and this guy from New York?" he asks casually on the ride back.

"He's coming in for Thanksgiving with his son and his mother. He's very close to his mother."

"How about his ex-wife?" Dusty asks. It just comes out.

"Why would his ex-wife come?"

"I meant, shouldn't you go there—New York or wherever the ex is—and talk to her before this thing goes any further?"

"Why would I do that?"

"Get a look at her, find out why they split up."

"She was impossible. You should hear the stories."

"They're all his stories. It would be interesting to get her side of it."

Dusty was teasing, of course. People don't interview ex-wives. Lily can't imagine herself having a chat with Foster's ex-wife about Foster. She can't really imagine her. Foster talks about her a lot, but when Lily tries to picture the ex-wife, she comes up with a cartoon. It's hardly possible that a woman could be that irrational. Driving home, Lily is sorry she even saw Dusty today. Instead of comforting her, Dusty kept disturbing her equilibrium, telling her that sad story and then showing her the clotted wound in the earth, reminding her of the dangers of love, how it can burn and sting and wring your guts out. Love can do that, touch a person at the weakest point, until the weakness consumes, until the person is no longer able to flourish or even to keep on. She doesn't want to meet Foster's wife ever.

It is dark and snowflakes are spinning before the headlights. When she reaches the top of her drive, she is happy to see lights on in the house and Dixie's ancient Toyota parked outside.

CHAPTER 11

■ ■ ■

Angel Day

DIXIE LOOKS UP from the sofa she's covering to see Louis standing on the other side. He often surprises her like this, suddenly appearing. Unlike most men in Priest Creek, who wear boots, so you can hear them coming a mile away, Louis wears Indian moccasins that whisper when he walks. On bad days, Louis's hair is gray string and his eyes are windows where there's no one home. But sometimes he can look like an angel, with his wavy blond hair to his shoulders and eyes that see straight into yours. This is an angel day.

"Jiminy Jaysus, Louis! You scare the pants off me when you do that."

He didn't mean to, he says. He holds the fabric so she can get the corner smooth and neat. Louis has a deformity. The last two fingers of his left hand are fused together. It gave Dixie the creeps when she first noticed it, then it fascinated her. Now she's used to it. It seems to help him in his work, as if his hand had been specifically modified for pleating and holding fabric smooth. She sometimes finds herself working with her own two fingers pressed tightly together.

"What was that song you were singing when I came in?" he asks.

"Some cracker tune I learned from my grammy back home." Louis's people are from Rhode Island. There are rumors that he has money, but if he had, why would he bother covering chairs? Whatever kind of place Louis is from, it's very different from Dixie's and he's always interested in her stories, which she exaggerates so much for him that sometimes she can't remember the way it really went.

"I saw Lily's truck going out to the airport." He stretches the fabric in place for her.

"Praise be Jaysus! That must mean Romeo's going home. I was wondering when he'd ever leave."

Louis continues helping Dixie, although she was doing fine by herself. "I guess you'll be going back to Lily's now."

Dixie's been making it look as if she's been staying at the shop even though she's been sleeping at Shane's. She keeps her car out front and has Shane come pick her up or Louis drop her at Shane's every night. She even has her sleeping bag on a sectional sofa in the back and her bag of clothes beside it. This isn't just for Lily—who hasn't been around at all since Foster came and probably hasn't thought once about Dixie—but for Shane as well. He appreciates Dixie more this way.

"Would you sing that song again?" Louis asks.

She changes the key so Louis can join in. It's a slow ballad, a little on the mournful side, a good tune to sing while you're working. The last time she and Louis sang together in the shop was before she made the mistake of trying to move in with him.

"You know, I thought I recognized it. The melody is Welsh, from the seventeenth century or before." Louis quickly sings her a verse in a tickly language. It gives her a lonesome feeling to think of all the people long gone who've sung the same song.

She's been feeling melancholy. It began last night. She made macaroni and cheese for Shane. He asked her to, although he knows she's making only healthy things and macaroni and cheese is full of fat and cholesterol. Afterward they made love. It was as if they'd died and come back to earth for the one perfect night they couldn't manage to have while they were alive.

Dixie woke this morning with a sadness on her and found herself singing all her grammy's old dirgy ballads. Having Louis beside her singing seemed like heaven to her once. Now it only makes her sadder.

The day she left Shane and moved in with Louis began this way, with Louis looking angelic and singing with her. They were working on the Petrillos' sofa, re-covering it with rose damask. They were close, like this, and Dixie turned her face so it was next to Louis's and he kissed her. They were just moving on from there when Judy Chow walked in. Before Judy left, someone else came in. Finally, Dixie and Louis were alone again. "You do the locking up," Louis told her, and then he was gone through the door that leads to his apartment over the shop. She listened to his moccasins, fast and light on the stairs, and wondered if she was supposed to follow. Then she heard the lock to his door going gently into place.

At the time, Shane was working nights over at Ski Haus, so he wasn't there when she got home. She fed Jewel. There wasn't much to eat, just some Pacificos and a half bag of Doritos. She must have fallen asleep in front of the TV, because she woke up and Shane was screaming at her, about how there wasn't any beer, there wasn't any food, the house was a pigsty. She was saying it wasn't a house but a goddamn pissant rented trailer. It was a fairly typical argument for them to have. The only thing different was that this time Dixie went in and packed her clothes. "Where do you think you're going?" he said. "There are plenty of people who'd be happy to have me," she said. It wasn't until she was in her car that she realized she was going to Louis.

When Dixie was growing up, her grammy and her ma

used to tell her she had too much imagination. It was only recently that Dixie learned that some people think imagination is a good thing. Dixie's more inclined to agree with her grammy. By the time she ran up the stairs to Louis's apartment with Jewel at her side, and her suitcase in her hand, she had traveled a long road. She could see Louis taking her in his arms. She would cook him Southern food. They'd have a baby who would stay in a playpen in the shop and watch them work. Every night they'd go home to a ranch on Conners Creek Road. Her imagination carried her across the doorsill. Her arms were around his neck before she read the message in his eyes and his arms hanging stiffly down. "It's just for a couple of days, a week or two, until I can find a place of my own," she told him.

Down here in the shop there is furniture everywhere, and it all has a place. You can tell at a glance when a piece will be finished by the spot it occupies on the floor. It took Dixie a while to discover this order and learn how to move things within the plan. It was the same upstairs, but instead of furniture, there were books—shelves of them and stacks on the floor. There was one metal kitchen table and one straight chair, one beat-up easy chair and hassock, one reading lamp. In the bedroom there were clothes hung on pegs around the room and a narrow bed. She had to persuade Louis to help her move a sofa up from the shop so she could sleep on it.

There was another room Louis kept locked and wouldn't let her see, but she found the key once when he was out. It was so bright at first that she couldn't take in what it was. The walls and ceiling were covered in Mylar and there were Gro-Lites making the room as bright as day even though the windows were boarded up. There were plants, like a miniature field, but there wasn't any dirt, because everything was growing in water. Louis had lined the floor with plastic and had rigged up plastic tubes to drip onto the roots. A fan blew the air around while a tape played classical music that was as strict and measured as the drops of water. Between his books and his marijuana, Louis had a complete life. He didn't need Dixie.

And yet many times in the shop she'd felt his body respond when she'd brushed up against him. He was a divided man—his body was downstairs and his head upstairs. She'd hoped to move his body upstairs as well. Instead, it worked the other way. The head came down to the shop and Louis kept his distance. The singing stopped. It's taken all this time to get him back to where he was before she moved in.

It wasn't her intention to get Louis's interest again. It was an accident, something she couldn't have planned because she would have thought it would have the opposite effect. Louis was out of the shop one day when Shane came in. Dixie took the sign with the paper clock on it, moved the hands to say she'd be back at two, and hung it on the door. She didn't hear Louis. She opened her eyes to see him looking down at them from behind the upturned legs of some dining chairs. Louis walked away on whispering feet. She never told Shane and Louis never said anything.

Since that day Louis began noticing her again, helping her with heavy pieces, brushing up against her accidentally on purpose. And today he is singing. His thigh presses against hers. They could put the paper clock in the door. They could use the sofa in the back where her sleeping bag is. Two years ago she would have done it, already seeing Louis on the porch of their mountain cabin. It's the way she's done everything all her life.

When she was eleven, the first time she packed to spend the summer with her father and his new wife, she folded her yellow shorts and T-shirt with the flowers on it and dreamed she would be wearing them the day her father asked her to stay forever. She did the same when she was twelve, thirteen, fourteen, and each year they sent her back exactly when they'd said they would. The last time she visited, the firemen's carnival was starting just hours after she was supposed to leave and they still made her go on that day. They couldn't understand how "such a great big girl" could cry and carry on so about missing a firemen's carnival.

When she'd moved in with Shane—his college degree, his cowboy posters—she thought it would be only a matter of months before they'd be sharing a cabin under the ponderosas. Now she can't even be sure of a place in his trailer.

She'd been trying to learn Creative Imaging, but it seems to be too much like what she's always done. She's beginning to think that the only lessons she can learn are not from what she reads or someone tells her but from what life hands her. And her lesson is be careful not to pack your dreams when you leave on a journey, even if it's only to a sofa in the back of the shop.

Louis is standing close. They could lock the door and pull the shade and finish what Judy Chow interrupted a long time ago. Dixie's body is already pulling her toward it while her mind is spinning through the what-will-happen-after possibilities. It's an angel day for Louis, his breath is in her hair, and she's thinking it's best to let things happen—to shake things up, because you never know what might fall out. It might be something good.

When Shane comes by the shop at one, the door is locked, even though the hands on the paper clock promise that it will open again at noon.

CHAPTER 12

The Superior Man
Receives a Carriage

CORDELIA IS part thoroughbred, part quarter horse, and half donkey. Lily presided over her conception and birth four years ago. The idea was to breed a mule with the surefooted agility of a donkey, the temperament of a quarter horse, and the gait of a thoroughbred. It worked, mostly, although Cordelia does have some thoroughbred skittishness to her. She overreacts. If she needs three feet to clear a stream, she'll jump six.

Lily is riding the fence line, hoping to repair any breaks before snow covers everything. She is snug in her long, oiled coat that extends over her saddle and down to her boots like a tent. Frozen pellets stick to Cordelia's mane, but the mule doesn't mind the cold. It's heat and flies that put her into a temper. Dixie's going to be disappointed that Lily didn't wait for the weekend so the two of them could make this ride as planned. When Lily saw the clouds piling in this morning, she decided she'd better get it done in case this was a big snow coming. She almost hopes it is, so she doesn't have to justify herself to Dixie. Dixie's funny—so careless and reckless in some ways and so finely tuned, so susceptible to being hurt in others. It can be annoying, having to worry about someone's feelings when you're only doing what you have to. Still, she'll admit she was happy to see Dixie's Toyota parked in front of the house when she drove up that night after saying goodbye to Foster. Foster left a loneliness behind, even though he is coming back Thanksgiving. It's the times Lily doesn't hear from him that she's thankful to have Dixie around.

Foster hasn't called in four days. Why can't she stop thinking about it? "It's not as if I needed him; it's not as if I went out looking for a man. He just showed up—" Lily was saying to Dixie last night at dinner. "Jiminy Jaysus, Lily, give him a call, why don't you? I'll do the dishes." Dixie poured herself the last of the wine, a Colorado rosé she'd brought home to try. Lily said she'd only get his machine and she hated talking to his machine.

Two fence posts are out, knocked down by hunters, maybe, chasing after elk. Lily rides over to investigate. The mule screams and wheels around, kicking her hind legs in the air. Lily digs her knees in and pulls back on the reins. The mule bellows, staggers, and before Lily can save herself, they are down—Lily on her back, the mule across her chest. Lily presses her face into the mule's neck to keep from getting hit in the head by a hoof when the animal rolls to its feet, but the moment doesn't come. After the frenzy, there is nothing.

Cordelia is alive—eyes swivel in sockets, breath heaves out in steamy clouds—but paralyzed. It takes Lily a while to figure out that the lead rope is caught under the mule so she can't move her head. If she can't move her head, she can't get up.

Cordelia must have walked into a piece of barbed wire from the downed fence. It got tangled in her legs and threw her into a panic. Lily feels the wire digging into her own leg, caught beneath the mule.

There's no sense calling for help. If anyone is nearby he would have heard the clamor and would be running to investigate. It is unlikely that anyone is near. In about an hour it will be dark. An hour after that, Dixie will get home. Lily left a note on the table, cryptic, but Dixie should know the route, approximately. Lily tries to picture Dixie taking the note off the table and reading it, but the image won't come. Dixie often returns late and sometimes not at all. As another precaution Lily left a message on Dusty's answering machine. But she doesn't know what Dusty is doing today, if he is even in town. She realized when she called that she hadn't heard from him since the ride to Sulfur Cave.

Eventually someone will find her, but probably not before tomorrow. It could snow all night. Every time Cordelia writhes in a futile attempt at getting free, barbed wire cuts into Lily's leg. On Cordelia's other side, the down side, is a saddlebag containing wire clippers, hopelessly beyond reach.

Gravy sits close to Lily's head and peers into her eyes, looking so worried, so anxious, so eager to help that Lily has to laugh. "Gravy, go get that extra pair of wire clippers. They're hanging in the barn, Gravy. Wire clippers." Gravy catches a string of saliva with her tongue and clouds Lily's face with dog breath.

Dusty glides through the slippery, medicinal, blood-warm water like a walrus—underwater, coming up for air and then down again, back and forth. He has the pool to himself. It can be crowded in summer, but on a chill November day with sleet squalls and freezing rain, outdoor swimming doesn't attract the multitudes.

These are the healing waters of the Utes, the same stinking springs where warriors bathed their wounds. Since the Utes were banished to the reservation, the springs have been dug out, decked over, forced to run into cement-bottom pools. Dusty has photos of the springs in all their transmutations. Marietta's father was responsible for this latest improvement: the commodious redwood building with lockers, showers, an indoor water slide and water jets, and this outdoor swimming pool—a long way from the natural springs. But Dusty can't complain—he's using it, isn't he?

He surfaces to cool his head and shoulders. It's snowing in heavy flakes. Late fall in Priest Creek is a season most tourists and second-home people avoid, but it's one Dusty's always enjoyed because it's filled with anticipation. All through town the saws are going, the hammers, getting ready for the skiers. The big topic of conversation is snow. "They got three inches up at the top last night," someone says in the Lost Dollar, and all down the bar heads nod in approbation. The collective wealth, the town treasure, is piling up on the mountain. Priest Creek never had gold or silver, good grazing, or a long enough growing season, but it always had snow. What would Bibleback make of it, this strange alchemy that turns snow to gold.

Dusty's beard is freezing. He submerges in his shadowy bath. It suits his lugubrious mood, as does the weather— nimbostratus clouds like a thick gray lid coming down over the valley.

Marietta wasted no time in contacting "toxic-waste people" from some outfit in Denver and making arrangements for them to come up and explore Sulfur Cave. It will be a miracle if they find Bibleback's twisted bones in there. Dusty has done everything he can to talk her out of it, but Marietta has more faith in Dusty's story than he does. She has taken Bibleback and Cora away from Dusty and made them her own.

Dusty went to see her in her restaurant at the top of the gondola. She's changing it from Chez Marietta to Cora Burtons, having real logs plastered to the walls, redoing the booths in cowhide. "I want it to look like a log cabin," she explained. She was dressed in plum calico with starched white petticoats. The restaurant will look as much like a log cabin as any place can that has triple-height ceilings and wraparound cantilevered window-walls. The menu will feature field-greens salad, root vegetables, corn bread, beans, and local game. Marietta wants Dusty to get AP, UPI, and CNN on site at the cave when the people with the moon suits go in for Bibleback's bones. Dusty is praying for a premature blizzard, one tremendous snow to bury the cave until Marietta's on to some new passion.

There are a couple of inches of slush on the road as Dusty, pink and pickled from his long swim, heads his truck down Main Street toward home. The healing springs did not change his mood, but they took the sting out, so now he's feeling pleasantly melancholy. A van passes, loaded with elk antlers on the roof rack. He counts ten. Inside the van are ten elk, reduced to seventy-five-pound crates of meat and hides. Ten mighty elk packaged to go out on the next plane. Usually it amuses Dusty when hunters arrive fresh from their executive offices in Dallas, New York, Boston, and go back with antlers in their luggage. Dusty makes money from the hunters. He rents One and Two out to Eden Glen for the season. He's looking forward to his share of the elk meat, which he makes into sausages. Today, however, the van with its bloody cargo looks obscene, reminds him that *Homo sapiens* is a very fucked-up animal.

He's hungry when he gets home, and thirsty. He has three thick slices of his sourdough rye and two beers before he remembers to check his machine for messages. The first three are from Marietta. He goes to the bathroom, then he hears Lily's voice on the machine. It's over by the time he comes out. He rewinds and patiently waits through Marietta until it comes back to Lily. She's out riding the fence line, she says, leaving at eleven, will be back by four.

He hasn't heard from Lily since the day lover boy flew

out and she came to Dusty for comforting. She's calling now in case something goes wrong on her solitary ride. She doesn't have to explain why she's giving Dusty this information, because she often tells him when she's riding alone, just in case, and then she calls when she gets in. Sometimes he'll find two messages on his machine—she's gone out, she's back. Thanks, Dusty, old friend, old pal, old eunuch, old shoe.

It is now 5:07. Lorraine is scratching at the door. He opens it to let her in. It's foul out there and dark, and Lily hasn't called. Being in love distracts her. She wasn't all there the day they rode to Sulfur Cave. He telephones her, but she doesn't answer—must be doing chores. He leaves a stern message on her machine to call him back instantly.

When Dusty wakes, it takes him a while to figure out where he is. His house is dark. He fell asleep in front of the television, watching the news—he remembers now—but the television is off. He hears the river, fat with rain and snow, roaring past his cabin. It's an urgent sound he never gets used to, reminds him how fast time passes, how people you love can be snatched away in a blink, a breath.

Dusty's mother disappeared when he was seven. She left him at school in the morning, but in the afternoon, when Dusty went to the place where she always picked him up, she wasn't there. She died in a head-on collision with a truck; she'd swerved to avoid a dog in the road. Dusty can't remember anyone telling him that—did he make it up? All he knows is that in the morning his mother was there and in the afternoon she was gone forever.

There's something he forgot to do, but what? Lorraine? He hears her nails click along the floor and feels her wet nose in his hand. What else? One and Two are safely locked away in Eden Glen's stables, chowing down on oats someone else is paying for. Then what? He feels around for the lamp and turns the switch, but nothing happens. Of course.

Lines must be down; that's why the TV isn't on. He picks up the phone. Dead. Phone. Lily. He asked her to call back but she can't if the line is dead. A lonesome feeling, to be in one's cabin without light. He fumbles around and gets his kerosene lanterns going. He cuts another slice of bread and chews thoughtfully. He could go to the Lost Dollar, see how they're managing with the electricity gone, scope out the extent of the power shortage.

He feeds Lorraine, spruces a bit in the mirror by the light of the lantern. When he gets in his truck, he thinks about swinging by Lily's to see if she's all right. Dixie will be there. They'll be having dinner, or just cleaning up, talking about men, laughing. He'll stand in the mudroom, unwilling or uninvited to take off his boots and go in. He'll say, "Uh, just stopped by to see if you were okay." Lily will look puzzled and then remember the message she left. "Oh right. Sure. Thanks, Dusty." When he closes the door there will be a fresh burst of laughter.

There are tracks in Lily's driveway. Looks like someone drove up, turned around, and drove out. In front of the dark house, curling around the barn, are drifts of unbroken snow. Back by four, she said. Three and a half hours ago. It's their code. She relies on him. She always calls to let him know.

From the chicken coop comes the eerie wail of the peacock. He scans the yard, the barn, with his flashlight. He goes in the house. A piece of paper left on the kitchen table reads: "Dixie, I'm up riding the fence. Back by four." He crumples it and throws it on the floor. Dixie did not come back to see the note and know what it meant: "If you see this, I'm in trouble." Because the one thing you can count on with Dixie is that if you need her she won't be there.

He finds the saddle and straps it on Simone, slips the bridle over her nose. She's uncommonly docile, as if she understands. The saddle's too small for him, the stirrups too short. He's not a heroic figure perched on this saddle, his legs drawn up, this man who slept in his chair while Lily was—God knows. He urges Simone over the path his headlamp makes across the snowy ground.

The nose of the mule could be a distant snow scene, the rime-coated hairs, fir trees covered with frost. This has been the extent of Lily's vision, the mule's whitened nose and the dog's anxious eyes. She can hear the mule and the dog breathing, the other dog whimpering, and snow hissing for miles around. An owl hoots; another, more distant, answers. She has been able to get her trapped arm out and has contrived to untangle the lead rope. She can, with one last movement, free Cordelia's head. The mule will heave to her feet and Lily will attempt to roll out of the way of the hooves. She doesn't know if she can. Her leg could be caught in the barbed wire. Will she be able to stand? She doesn't know. She is taking a moment to listen to snow and owls; she's dallying before focusing on the essential.

Her father lost his concentration while driving alone, back from the country club late at night, and went over an embankment. Lily, home for the funeral, went to look at the place. She thought if she saw it—the tire marks on the road where her father jammed on the brakes, the broken guardrail—she could tell why. But all she could tell was the path the car made. Lily blamed her mother for being cool at the funeral, in command of herself and those around her. Lily recalled the vacations her mother sometimes went off on, how her father would then stay out at the club too late and not be able to make it upstairs to his bed; Lily would find him sleeping on the sofa the next morning.

Later, Lily wished her mother had been as icy and remorseless as she had seemed on the day of the funeral—at least she would have been able to care for herself. In fact, she had already started on her own path downward —sleeping pills at night, an antidepressant for day, a bloody Mary at lunch, then wine, a couple of whiskeys after dinner.

The failure to grab hold, to accept responsibility for being alive, could be genetic. What if Lily is the last of a bad strain. What if for all her outward strength something lurks in her DNA, a fatal weakness that in the crucial moment loosens the will to live, and she lets herself over the edge? She rode Cordelia to the downed fence, knowing there would be barbed wire lying loose. She always dismounts as soon as she sees there's a fence down. Always. And yet this time it was as if the barbed wire, lurking unseen in the weeds, pulled her toward it. Her mind was on Foster. What if there is something in her blood that renders love a lethal emotion?

Cordelia snorts and struggles to lift her head. Lily wrenches the rope and throws herself back as the mule lurches. A hoof connects with Lily's cheek. She sits on the ground holding her head. Her hands tell her something is wrong with her face, but she feels nothing, not even the touch of her hands. Without thinking about whether her legs will work or not, Lily is up, running after Cordelia, trying to get around to the front of her so as not to get caught in the wire. The dogs are barking. Cordelia's braying, and then nothing. The mule has disappeared.

Lily thinks it's her mind at first, that part of her own mind is missing, not the mule. She follows the dogs to a sinkhole about twelve feet deep and twenty feet across. It takes her a while to see and understand that the mule has fallen into it and landed on her back, her legs in the air. She is stunned but breathing. The saddle is wedged into a log; that's what is holding her in this unnatural position. Lily gets the clippers out of the saddlebag and cuts the wire off Cordelia's legs. They are torn and bloody but seem sound. Holding the log with her foot, Lily puts her shoulder to the mule and pushes her over. Cordelia clambers to her feet, meek and trembling. Lily takes the rope and leads her up the bank.

She's been walking months, miles, or has only begun—she can't tell—when she hears Simone whinny. Cordelia answers. A light wavers through the snow.

"You shouldn't let a mule step on your face, Lily."

"Looks bad, huh?"

"You've looked better."

Dusty's driving her to the medical center. First she made him call the vet, who said Cordelia was probably all right, since she managed to walk home. Lily had to talk to the vet herself because she didn't trust Dusty, who was in a panic to get to the medical center. In Dusty's heated truck, with nothing to do but sit, Lily gives herself over to the pain. It fills her head, fills the cab, presses against the windshield in voluptuous surges, pushing out other thoughts. Foster hasn't called. That's a thin and distant fact, hardly discernible through the enveloping pain. She can understand how someone might purposely harm himself (van Gogh cut off his ear) to release his mind from an oppressive rut.

Dusty's hand closes over hers. "Hang on, kid. Almost there."

Lily watches snow whirling in a backward vortex out of some dark center.

Dusty helps Lily to bed. She's drugged for pain, stitched up—one leg's a mess; she'll have to go to Denver for plastic surgery on her face when she feels up to it. She asks Dusty to look in on Cordelia and make sure she's all right.

The mule is long in the leg like her mother, and has the same diamond on her forehead. Dusty told Lily it was a waste to mate a mare with good bloodlines and a donkey. Lily went ahead anyway and came up with the most elegant mule you'd hope to see. He removes the feedbag he hung over her nose earlier and inspects her legs. The back ones are bloody and torn, but they don't look as bad as Lily's leg. And the mule's face is untouched. Clearly, Lily got the worst of it. The mule nudges him with her nose. He scratches between her eyes. Would he be caressing her now if she had come home dragging Lily's body wrapped in barbed wire? An innocent brute, blameless as a dog in the middle of the road. Dusty breaks up a bale and pitches some hay into her stall. He feels a slight twinge, a barely noticeable urge to take the pitchfork and knock the beast right between the eyes, to crack open the white diamond, but he doesn't.

Lily never buys hard liquor, only an occasional bottle of wine, and beer, of course. Dusty keeps a bottle of Canadian Club here, but it is not in its usual place. He finds it at last. Lover boy must have been into it. Dusty splashes some over ice and goes out on the deck. The wind has died down and the snow is falling softly, inexorably. If Lily had been knocked unconscious, if the hoof had hit just a little differently, the snow would have covered her body by now. Snow that Dusty wished for, snug and lazy in his house, worrying about Marietta, his own small problems, while Lily lay pinned under the goddamned mule.

Dusty swallows the whiskey and looks up at the sky, heavy overhead like the inverted hand of God. After a while he goes inside to find some more whiskey and Lily's sleeping bag. He spreads the bag on the floor in front of the stove. Lily's books are mostly practical volumes that have to do with ranching. On the higher shelves are the books you find in anyone's library, anyone who's had a liberal arts education, books everyone intends to read again sometime and never gets around to. You could find a Bible in among such books, the relic of some survey of religion course, but there isn't one here. Dusty was hoping to find a Bible, open it at random, and flush out an answer. He finds the *I Ching* instead and comes up with this message to ponder:

> There is a large fruit still uneaten.
> The superior man receives a carriage.
> The house of the inferior man is split apart.

CHAPTER 13

. . .

The House Split Apart

USED TO BE after a week on the mountain, the Eden Glen hands would go straight to the Lost Dollar and buy rounds for the whole place. There'd be music, dancing, usually a fight or two. They'd get home, paychecks half gone, when the sun was coming up. The women understood. It was part of elk season. You're supposed to look like you're having a good time, but taking hunters out is a job. You're babysitting grown men. Half of them can't even put up their own tent. You cook their dinner, wash their dishes, practically wipe their noses for them. And don't forget the horses—saddling, grooming, feeding. You're on good behavior all week. No matter what guests say or do, you have to be courteous, friendly but professional. Afterward you're ready for some bad behavior.

But this time everyone went home. Wouldn't even stop for a beer. Because of the snow and the power being down. And the women aren't as understanding as they used to be. So Shane is alone at the Lost Dollar. The kerosene lanterns on the bar just make things spooky and sad. They need a generator here like they have at the medical center for when the power goes down. What's a bar without a jukebox or a TV? It wouldn't be so bad if there were someone to talk to, but nobody's here. The bartender's down at the other end talking to two customers who look like college students. Shane's never seen them before, or the guy tending bar. They looked at Shane when he first came in wearing his chaps and boots, and he figured they'd try to strike up a conversation. Sometimes the kids who work on the ski mountain come down to the Lost Dollar to find a real cowboy to talk to. Shane might have let them buy him a beer. But they looked just long enough to satisfy their curiosity and went back to talking with each other.

"Has Dusty been in tonight?" Shane calls to them. "You know him, don't you, kind of stocky, always wears a hat? How about Dixie? You know her? Any women been in tonight?"

"Nobody's been in and I don't think anybody's coming in either. I was just closing up," the bartender says.

You'd think Shane had been gone a year instead of a week—strangers in the Lost Dollar—don't know him or his friends—kids who think they own the place. "If it isn't too much trouble, sonny, I'd like a six-pack of Pacifico to go."

"All I got is bottles."

"Give me bottles, then."

No sense in going home, where there isn't any water, heat, or lights. He'll go to Lily's. She'll have kerosene lanterns and a wood stove going. Lily won't be overjoyed to see him, but she won't turn him out in the cold.

He thinks it's strange that there aren't any tracks in Lily's driveway, meaning no one's been up or out since it started snowing, but he still isn't prepared for the dark house. His headlights pick up Lily's truck, covered with snow. It's odd that they took that old Toyota of Dixie's in this weather, but that was before it started snowing—otherwise he would have seen the tracks. Shane turns back toward town, half expecting to see Dixie's car coming the other way.

When he was a little kid, someone gave him a sugar Easter egg decorated with icing on the outside, with one end open so he could look in and see a boy and girl rabbit skipping along a road to a sugar palace. There were hedges of flowers, a bird flying over, a complete world. Now, what made him think of that egg? How can a memory stay buried so long and then pop up so clear? It must be the way the snow is covering the windshield, white like the sugar shell of that egg, and the rounded opening the windshield wipers make. Somehow he got the idea that the rabbits inside the egg were moving around when he wasn't looking. He'd sneak up on the egg and peek inside to catch them at it. He slept with a flashlight so he could surprise them in the middle of the night. He held the egg up to his mouth and whispered, pleaded, promised he wouldn't tell. He shouted, to make them jump. He squeezed the egg in both hands— the powdery breath of it—sugar shards and scraps of paper.

There's Rick Starrett parked at the intersection with his bubble light going, warning people who might be coming through that there's a crossroad here, that this is a town, because without lights you'd never guess. Rick's the first person Shane's seen tonight whom he knows. He raises his hand on the steering wheel in greeting, even though the gesture will be lost in the snow between them.

The Safeway parking lot and the two trailers behind it no longer exist. It's a blank. Nothing says there are homes there, not a track or a trail, not a light. It makes Shane feel like a ghost or, worse, someone who never was. He thought Dixie might have been there looking for him or Frankie. Sometimes she takes care of Frankie when it's convenient. The kid worships her. He cringes when he sees Shane, although Shane has never laid a hand on him. Shane almost does want to hit him when the kid cringes like that. Those trailers aren't real homes anyway. They're more like containers, human dumpsters.

Main Street has been cleared; the highway crew have come and gone. They've cleaned out the parking places and piled snow down the middle of the street in the usual way, but the parking spots are empty. Nobody's on the sidewalks. The stores, the restaurants, the bars sit behind the falling snow, closed up and inscrutable. It's as if the whole town had gotten a message Shane failed to hear, and they left when his back was turned. He knows where they are—home in front of their wood stoves, toasting bread and cheese and boiling pots of hot chocolate, every isolated nest a world of its own. Even Jim Cosby has a wood stove. Shane thinks about going up there—he forgot to give him back the gun—but Jim's kids are always screaming and the place smells of dirty diapers. What he would really like to find, what he's been looking for, is Dixie's car stuck somewhere with Lily and Dixie in it. He'd like to rescue them. He'd like to hear his name called out in pleasure and relief.

On the hunting trip he got used to being needed. It can be a pain, but it can be good too, having a neurosurgeon from Atlanta depending on you to tell him where to stand to get his elk. Shane was carrying Jim's .30-06, because all the Eden Glen hands are supposed to be crack shots, standing by to anchor a wounded elk if the guest bungles it. Luckily, Shane didn't have to use the gun. The neurosurgeon took a big buck at one shot, dropped him in his tracks. The surgeon and his buddy, who has his own company in New York City, grew up together in Texas. They knew guns and horses, didn't require as much babysitting as the others. The one from New York—Conway was his name—told Shane what his company did, something with satellites, communications, government permissions. Shane didn't understand half of what he was talking about. Conway was younger than Shane too.

Shane's used to being younger than the guests. It gave him an odd feeling—if Dusty had been at the Lost Dollar he would have liked to discuss it with him. When the guests were older, Shane always felt like the promising young guy who could be persuaded to join a guest's business—probably wouldn't, but if the offer was right . . . Now here was this younger man, Conway, already a big shot in a business Shane couldn't even understand. It made Shane feel passed over, obsolete, that his future had run out.

After the first day Conway stopped talking about business. It usually happens that way. Everyone gets into riding with the gun strapped behind the saddle and watching for signs of elk. The last night, Shane told the Texans his story, how he gave up everything to come to P. Creek and lead the life he wanted. It's one he likes to tell guests who have to go back to some office on Monday, who are wondering how Shane escaped all that. This time it came out different, however, and it didn't seem like Shane gave up that much, or that he got that much, for that matter.

Almost everyone in P. Creek gave up a regular career to come here. There are schoolteachers driving vans to the airport, CPA's giving ski lessons—no big deal. Louis must have given something up, but he never says what. He has lots of books—Dixie told Shane that. She also told him about Louis's private pot farm, how he's turned on all the time.

Just before Shane left on the Eden Glen trip, he stopped by Louis's shop to say goodbye to Dixie. He was still thinking about how nice it was the night before, and he was hoping to find her alone. But the door to the shop was closed and the shade drawn. The paper clock in the window said they'd be back at noon, but it was after one and Shane couldn't wait.

He doesn't know why he thought to look for her car at Louis's, but it's here, parked in the back, and it looks as if it's been here all day, before the snow began. It looks as if it's taken up residence.

He wasn't angry the time Dixie left to go live with Louis. He was relieved, if anything, to get her out of his place.

Then the Eden Glen boys, Jim Cosby especially, started teasing him about it, about how Louis had stolen his woman away from him, when he knew it wasn't like that. He never held it against Louis personally, especially since Dixie had told him Louis had something wrong with him. He assumed Louis couldn't get it up.

Does this mean Louis can get it up and they're getting it on? Or maybe Lily got fed up and kicked her out. It could be all of the above.

Shane is parked in front of Louis's, finishing a beer. Before he left on the trip, he told her he was coming back tonight and that she could find him at the Lost Dollar. She said it wasn't a whole lot of fun to stand around in a bar with a bunch of smelly wranglers talking about a trip she hadn't been on.

She's back with Louis. Shane's been out only one week and his favorite bar is filled with strangers and his woman is sleeping with someone else. His home, the dumpster, is cold and dark. If he went back to Minneapolis, he'd find his wife married to someone he never met, with kids he's never seen—two, he thinks. His place on earth has shrunk down to this truck with three empty bottles of beer and three full, his saddle and bags, and Cosby's .30-06.

He gets out to release a hissing stream of urine. Light is spilling out the windows over the shop, making halos in the snowy air. They've got at least three kerosene lanterns going and a wood stove; he can smell the piney smoke. Holding a beer in one hand, negotiating slippery steps, Shane notices he's in a state of having had one too many. He straightens himself out a little before he knocks. There's a rustling, but nobody comes to the door.

"Hey, it's Shane. Open up."

He hears her and he knows just what she looks like, laughing and holding her hands over her mouth, like a little kid.

Going down the stairs, he curses, and the bottle slips out of his hand and breaks on something below. He sees the gun in the truck and thinks that he could scare them with it, just to get even for not opening the door on a snowy night. These boots are not the right thing for climbing stairs in the snow. He should be wearing his Sorels.

"Hey! Open up! I want to talk to you."

What he hears is an absence of sound, a holding breath and waiting stillness. He has frightened them. They must have been watching from the window when he took out the gun. Shane is not a gun person, not at all. A couple of times he fooled around with the gun up at Jim's, trying to shoot cans off a fence, and he hardly ever got one.

The two Texans, Conway and the neurosurgeon, could shoot. They knew guns. You could tell by the way they swung them to their shoulders and sighted down the barrel. "I gave it all up to live out here," Shane told them, sitting by the fire on the last night. "Just what did you give up," Conway asked, winking at his buddy, "besides your name? Shane isn't your real name, is it? What's your real name?" Conway kept needling, but Shane just ignored him. You mess things up with a guest and Eden Glen will never ask you back. Shane tries not to let guests get to him. In fact, he didn't even think about what Conway said until right now. He's thankful he didn't have to deal with a wounded elk, because he's a bad shot and Conway is the kind of guy who won't let you forget something like that. "What's the matter, *Shane*, didn't you ever shoot a gun before?" Shane knows just how he'd say it, emphasizing the name as if there was something funny about it.

It doesn't take a crack shot to get this lock on Louis's door. Shane has been holding the gun on it, thinking about it, and before he knows it—*kaboom*—the gun butt slams into his shoulder, so he has to grab the rail or he'd fall down the stairs. The shot brings a load of snow off the roof. There's a mountain of snow between him and the door, which is open now, sighing sugary marijuana breath.

He'd imagined Dixie and Louis filling up the room, but he has to study awhile before he locates them, crumpled on the floor in a way that reminds Shane of animals caught in their den—timid animals, rabbits maybe. One of them is hurt, or both. It's hard to tell because they're so tangled up together, but there's a lot of bright red blood.

Shane's driving. She's holding Louis between them. Shane had her go up and get some blankets to keep Louis from going into shock. Shane tied up Louis's hand and put a tourniquet around his arm. Shane's had Red Cross training. He took a course a couple of years ago. He thought he should, because on those Eden Glen trips you never know. He's never had to use it before tonight. She and Louis were in a daze. Shane had to find towels, Louis's jacket, and get him to the truck. He almost says that they were lucky he came along when he did, and then he remembers. Nobody is talking about what happened, but they must be thinking about it, and when they get to the clinic they'll say it.

"It was an accident," he says. "If you would've just opened the door, that's all you would've had to do."

When Shane was a kid he thought the sky was a dome above the earth, a shell protecting it from whatever lay outside. It took him the longest time to give up that idea. Even now, driving into the snow—so much snow—he gets the feeling that it isn't falling from clouds but that it's spewing out of a crack, a split in the sky dome, hurling at them, bringing all the wailing misery of what's beyond.

"Get him to shut up, can't you?" he tells her.

CHAPTER 14

■ ■ ■

The Flying Ram

DUSTY WALKS OUT of Lily's house and scans the pre-dawn sky, looking for obscurity in the west, signs of a snowstorm that's supposed to be coming in from Utah, as big as or bigger than the one that began the day of Lily's accident. Priest Creek could use it, as there hasn't been snow since then. People are canceling reservations for Christmas, switching to Sun Valley or Jackson, places where they've had steady accumulations. Dusty has his own reason for wanting snow: it could close the airport for days, keep Foster grounded in Denver, discourage him, thwart the impulse that made him decide at the last minute and without warning to fly out to see Lily. Dusty squints at the sky over the barn, willing the opacity of low-hanging clouds, but he sees an insolent star winking back at him from bottomless space.

Meanwhile, the raucous morning song has begun in the chicken coop. Dusty passes the breeding pen where the ewes are kept. Normally they stand mute, but today there's a disturbance, a thudding of hooves, a boiling of backs, with the sweeping horns of the mouflon ram floating through. Dusty stops to admire this descendent of the wild sheep of Sardinia—an ancient breed rooted in mythology—this bearer of the golden fleece, messenger from Zeus. The ram dances beside a ewe, cutting her off from the others, shoulders her to the fence, and climbs her back.

It has been two weeks since Dusty moved in with Lily.

He flew with her to Denver, where she had plastic surgery on her face. He took her to the medical center to have the stitches removed from her leg. Every day he works beside her, helping with the chores; every night he sleeps alone on the opposite side of the house. Last night, as they sat watching the satellite picture of the snowstorm churning toward Colorado like a smear of egg white across the map, he slid his hand across her shoulder and caught a strand of hair between his fingers. She pulled away as if he'd touched a wound, said she was tired, and went upstairs before he could wonder just what he had intended by taking her hair in his hand.

The ram releases the ewe; she trots off to join the others. Abruptly Dusty remembers his own role in this drama and seizes a pole that is leaning against the side of the barn. "Out! Get! Vamoose!" He shakes the pole at the ram, who clears the fence easily and, with a disdainful glance at Dusty, lopes down the hill. All the rams have been rigged with marking harnesses for the rutting season. Dusty sees, on his way back from the chicken coop, that a second ewe also wears the violet stripes of the mouflon.

Hours before his usual time, Foster hauled himself out of bed, causing his sinuses to click with a tinny sound, making him question why he was putting himself through this. But there was a car and driver at the door to take him to the airport and a prepaid ticket waiting for him, and at that hour it seemed easier to go with the plan than to try to change everything. Dusty hadn't been exactly cordial when Foster had called last night with the news that he was coming out—claimed Lily was sleeping, although it was only nine-thirty their time.

Originally, Foster had been going to take Bella and Nicholas to Lily's for Thanksgiving, but because of the accident, they'd canceled their plans. Bella had seemed more relieved than disappointed. She'd been enthusiastic about Lily when she was a distant fantasy, but the prospect of actually being in Lily's home had been making Bella anxious. She'd even had Foster go through her closet with her and choose appropriate clothes for the visit. (There were none.)

Foster would have flown out alone as soon as he heard about Lily's injuries, but only because he thought he should. He's squeamish about doctors, stitches, surgery. He was happy enough to have Dusty move in and see Lily through it. This is probably why he pushed away any concerns he had about Dusty and Lily living together, until yesterday, when he was having lunch with Meg and she said, "Is that good-old-boy of hers still living there? I would have thought she could make it on her own by now." Two weeks was a long time for a man and woman to sleep in separate beds in the same house. Foster and Lily hadn't lasted even one night. After lunch, Foster went over his work schedule to see if he could clear some time. The next thing he knew, he was booked on a flight to Priest Creek.

Now he's sitting on the New York to Denver plane, which is stalled on the runway for unexplained reasons; he isn't certain he'll make his connecting flight; he suspects that Dusty never gave Lily the message. He wonders what it is inside him that has forced him out here at the hour when ordinarily he would be waking up. Jealousy? Love? Or is it the fear of losing a connection to something he hasn't named?

"The problem is, the fence should be higher," Dusty tells Lily. They are standing in front of the pen where the ewes are kept.

"I'm not putting up a seven-foot fence just to keep some horny ram out."

"But the lambs will be good, won't they? He's a fine-

looking animal. It's survival of the fittest, isn't it? Of all
the rams, this one had the stuff to get over the fence."

Lily is recording the marks in her notebook. She's put
her best Manx ram in there, but so far he isn't showing
much enthusiasm. Dusty claims the other ram's marks are
discouraging him. "I promised some purebred Manx lambs
to a rancher in New Mexico," she tells Dusty. "If I left
everything to nature I'd have a mess. This isn't what I
planned."

"You aren't going to kill him, are you?"

"You don't have to watch." She goes in for the .22, gets
the cartridges off a high shelf, and loads the gun. On the
way out, she checks the sky for signs of the storm that's
supposed to be coming in. Flat clouds hovering just over
the barn could develop into something.

"Which way did he go? Did you see, Dusty?"

"Not really."

"They usually hang out by the creek this time of day."
She heads down the drive.

"Wait for me."

"You're not coming to throw off my aim, are you?" she
asks. Dusty looks hurt. She touches his back. He puts his
arm around her shoulder. They walk this way, clumsily.
There's been constraint between them recently, while before all was natural and easy. Last night Dusty caught his
hand in her hair and she pulled away, retreated to her
room. Sitting on her bed, her heart beating fast, she could
feel disappointment seeping up through the floorboards.
The phone rang. She knew it was Foster by the sound of
Dusty's voice when he answered. By the time she picked
up the extension, Foster had hung up. Why didn't she go
down to Dusty and ask him if it was Foster and if he was
calling from home? Why didn't she call Foster back? Because that incident with Dusty had thrown everything off.
Dusty has yet to mention that Foster called.

Both Lily and Dusty know that he is staying past the
time when she needs him; she could manage on her own,
but he doesn't leave and she doesn't suggest it. His presence
in her house anchors her mind and keeps it from drifting
back into what happened. It's not the moment when the
mule fell across her chest that she can't face, or the crack
of the hoof against her face. It's what led up to it, the blank
space in her thoughts when she rode over to the fence where
she knew the barbed wire would be lying coiled and hidden
in the weeds.

Dusty turns his head, then quickly looks away. She sees
what he saw, the ram, standing free and clear, almost pos-
ing, with his forelegs on a mound, his proud chest and
head as still as marble carved by an ancient knowing hand.

Dusty wraps the dead ram in a tarp and dumps it in the
back of his truck. The sound it makes reminds him of
another body hitting the metal so hard that it made Buzzy
raise his eyebrows.

"Have Max save the head," Lily says.

"What?"

"The head. I want to nail it to the side of the barn."

"Right." It will look good when the flesh has fallen away
and the curving horns are bleached to white. The body
rattles as the truck bounces over the ruts in Lily's drive.
That other time, with Lily beside him in the truck, calm
but pale, Dusty had taken care not to let the body slide or
bounce. His concern wasn't for the corpse, which couldn't
break.

The truck hits a pothole and the body jumps. Dusty
imagines Foster back there, wrapped in a tarp, on the way
to Bill Pease's funeral home. On occasion Bill Pease has to
prepare a body for burial, then crate it to be shipped home
in the belly of the Dash 7. Priest Creek is not Disneyland,
after all. Tourists sometimes are killed—riding accidents,

skiing accidents, climbing mishaps. Dusty stops himself. These thoughts are pleasant but unproductive. What Dusty has to do, as Lily's oldest and closest friend, is talk to Foster and explain to him that Lily can't be loved in a casual way, on a vacation schedule. Dusty isn't going to blame Foster—after all, Dusty's had plenty of short-term, ad hoc relations with women—just let him know the way it is with Lily. He'll pick Foster up at the airport and take him over to the Coyote, buy him a beer, have a quiet talk with him, and then Foster can stay at the Sheraton and leave in the morning. She'll never know he came.

Lily checks her answering machine—nothing from Foster —and wishes she'd gone with Dusty, who was odd, insisting that she stay home and rest. She calls Foster and gets his machine with the message that he'll be away for several days—must be what he wanted to tell her last night. She should tackle some of her bills and correspondence, but instead she wanders through her house as if in the home of a stranger, waiting for something, she doesn't know what.

In her bedroom, she takes off her clothes and stands before the mirror. She has become used to the way her face looks—the surgeon said the scars will fade eventually— but the red track curling up her leg shocks her. When Doc stitched the cut, Dusty held Lily's hand, talking easily and calmly, but his eyes were saying something else. She tries to imagine Foster looking at it. She touches it—smoother than skin—and wonders if he'll ever see it, or if he'll gradually stop calling and promising to come and the scar will grow over with—not quite skin—but something less sensitive to the touch.

Dusty shopped for groceries, picked up the mail, delivered the ram to Max's butcher shop. Max had his assistant take it to the back while he went out front with Dusty to look at the sky and wonder out loud where that storm went to. Max remarked that the plane from Denver was coming in right on schedule, a sign that the storm must have missed Priest Creek altogether. The assistant brought out the ram's head rolled in the tarp. Dusty unwrapped it and set it in the back of the truck. Max agreed that it was going to look fine on the side of Lily's barn.

The head slides across the truck bed as Dusty takes the turn, a little too fast, onto the airport road.

Foster is looking for the white pickup. It's some time before he realizes that the battered green pickup at the curb is flashing its headlights for him. He peers into the side window and sees Dusty, impassive behind his beard. Foster signals that he's going to put his bag in the back. He doesn't know what it is at first: a wadded, bloody cloth or rag, he thinks, until he sees the stony eyes. He falls back, clutching his bag to his stomach. A man and his young son turn to look. Foster gestures to the head. The boy seems interested, but the father pulls him on. Is Foster making too big a deal out of this? Is it customary here to show up at the airport with a severed head in the back of your truck? He thinks he sees Dusty grinning at him through the rear window, but when Foster opens the door and hauls his bag in with him, Dusty looks so solemn that Foster wonders if he imagined it. "I didn't realize it was you at first. I was looking for Lily's truck," he says.

Dusty eases out from the curb.

"She's all right, isn't she?" Foster asks after a while.

"She's all right, considering."

"That was some story—kicked in the face by a mule. She sounds good, though—over the phone. How does she look?"

"Like she got kicked in the face by a mule." Dusty turns abruptly off the road to Lily's and onto the approach to the ski area. Foster opens his mouth to say something, then doesn't. His breath is coming out in white frozen puffs. Isn't there heat in this truck? Dusty, in a parka and those sheepskin-lined boots they all wear out here, probably isn't feeling the cold. Foster is wearing a leather jacket and thin-soled loafers. It's been mild in New York and he forgot it was winter. He hugs his bag to his chest.

Dusty drives through the nearly empty parking area and stops in front of the Howling Coyote. He goes in, taking the keys with him. Foster watches skiers trudging over bare frozen ground to their cars. The lot empties out. Across from the gondola, the lights come on in the rooms of the Sheraton Hotel, one by one, and yet the place still looks deserted. Lily said the lack of snow was keeping tourists away. He's shivering, he realizes. He can either stay in the truck and freeze to death or join Dusty in the bar.

The Howling Coyote has the look of a place built for crowds: draft beer in paper cups, hamburgers and tacos served cafeteria style, big video screens showing skiers looping down virgin slopes. The voice of Ray Charles is wailing "Hit the Road, Jack" through the sound system. All that is missing is the crowd. There is only a huddle of drinkers at the bar. Foster takes the stool next to Dusty, who doesn't look his way but orders a Canadian Club on the rocks for him.

Foster, stirring his drink with the plastic straw, marvels at his own passivity. Several times he's looked over at the pay phone in the back and considered calling Lily. Is she aware that Dusty is holding Foster hostage? Does she even know that Foster is in town? As he listens to Dusty talking to these people, telling tales of winters past, acting like everyone's favorite uncle, the feeling deepens that he, Foster, has no place here. He steals a look at Dusty, burly-looking with his sleeves rolled up, his hat pushed back, and wonders what Dusty has been doing for Lily—lifting her? Changing her bandages? What if Lily has been hurt worse than she's let on and she needs more care than Foster can give her?

Dusty hears his own voice expounding on the effects of global warming on the jet stream—making it up as he goes along, stalling for time. The others keep looking at Foster nursing his drink, maintaining his cool. Dusty, a man of many words, cannot deliver the simplest sentence to him. The little talk he invented in the truck seems absurd now. Is it Dusty's place to protect Lily from someone who came all the way out here to see her? What right does Dusty have to keep Lily penned up? Dusty drains his glass and leaves. Foster follows.

Dusty has been checking his house regularly to make sure the pipes don't freeze. It's a lucky thing he came by tonight, because it's cold as a barn in here. He would have had ice on the floor by morning. He gets a good blaze going in the wood stove and draws himself up close. Some Canadian Club, no ice this time, will help. The cold of the room presses against his back. He turns on the TV in time to see the satellite picture of the storm coming across the border from Utah, pivoting around Priest Creek, and settling over Aspen and Vail. Weather is a chaotic system. It hinges on accidents.

Dusty went into Lily's house before Foster. "You took a long time," she said. She was in the kitchen getting dinner ready. "I stopped at the Coyote. Everyone's bummed out about the snow—" He heard Foster coming in behind him. Lily's hand went to her face. Foster stepped forward and took her hand so he could examine her temple. "It's not bad," Foster said. "I was expecting worse." As Dusty drove away, he remembered the head. He got out and stuck it up on a fence post by Lily's door.

"Do you want dinner?" Lily asks.

"God, yes, I'm starving," he says, and they laugh at themselves on the floor in the nest of clothes and afghan and pillows they pulled off the sofa. She puts her sweater on and finds the casserole she was taking out of the oven when Foster arrived.

Foster, the afghan draped across his shoulders, follows her. "Christ. That's some wicked wound you've got on your leg."

Lily flushes. She'd forgotten the scar.

"It adds to your mystique." He folds her into the blanket with him.

"I should heat this up. It's ice-cold."

"No, come on, we'll sit on the floor and eat out of the pan."

Lily turns on the TV so they can see whatever happened to that storm they were supposed to get, but when she comes back, she wants him to love her again. She sinks down next to him while the blue light from the television flickers across their bodies and the clouds ripped from the storm that never came hurl above the roof.

Foster reaches for someone, not quite aware, in his sleep, of who, and finds her missing. He opens his eyes, props himself up with pillows so he can see out the windows to the mountains and the mountainous, tumbling clouds. Lily's in the barn doing chores and he should be there helping, but he lingers for five minutes, then ten, partly because he has nothing suitable to wear—he doesn't know what he was thinking when he packed—and partly because he's a little shy about coming face to face with her in the daylight after last night. A ludicrous picture comes to mind, of pants around ankles, socks half off. He groans, rolls over, and grabs a pillow. He wants her again.

He waits. Time passes; Lily doesn't return. He finds some clean underwear in his bag and, shivering, goes downstairs. His clothes and hers are strung in a trail from the kitchen to the living room. He finds it disturbing that she left it this way, although he can't say why, as Lily's casual house-keeping has never bothered him before. It's a feeling that something has come undone; it's mixed up with her bat-tered face and the scar on her leg. He pulls on the clothes he wore last night, folds hers neatly and leaves them on a chair.

On the opposite side of the house, in the upstairs bath-room, Dusty's toiletries, his comb, deodorant, toothbrush, are all in place. The rumpled bed is material evidence that the poor bastard never slept in Lily's room. Foster finds a quilted coverall hanging in the closet and pulls it on over his city clothes. He has to roll the bottoms up, and the crotch comes halfway to his knees, but it will do. Dressed in Dusty's clothes, Foster feels a tenderness toward the man, much as he would toward a wounded animal. He switches his loafers for Dusty's workboots, a size too large.

Outside, it's sunny in spite of the clouds. Clownish in his getup, he shuffles toward the barn, already smiling at what Lily will say. A feeling that someone is watching him makes him stop and turn to meet the eye of an enormous bird, black from its curving beak to its feet—a raven. They're common here; he's seen them hopping around parking lots and garbage bins, but never this close. He moves silently forward for a better look. Although the wind ruffles its feathers, the bird fixes its eye on him, in warning or accusation, and doesn't stir. Foster stops, unnerved by the creature's refusal to fly away. Then he sees why: it is feeding and doesn't want to abandon its meal, a ram's head impaled on the post. The raven is eating out the eyes.

CHAPTER 15

• • •

The Last Roundup

The Last Roundup is a new store that sells vintage Western wear, the kinds of things Roy and Dale wore in the fifties, plus some genuine antiques from the turn of the century. Owner Nadine Halprin has been scouring the West for her finds and is eager to show them off. "Tell everybody it's okay if they just want to come in and look," she says. So be sure to stop in and see Nadine in her new store, tucked in beside Sore Saddles on Paradise Road. You can admire the giant tumbleweeds hanging from the ceiling and maybe pick out a cowboy boot mug for your morning coffee. It's something to do while you're waiting for snow.

—from the Priest Creek *Crier*

"YOU KNOW, Louis, you are a good-looking man. I can't understand why you don't spend more time on your personal appearance. It would make a difference. You would be happier if you'd just dress a little better." Dixie is going through Louis's clothes to find something he can wear to Marietta's party. Dixie has decided they should go—Dixie, Louis, and Shane together—because, as she explained it to Louis and Shane separately, there are all kinds of rumors going around. The other day Frankie asked

Dixie point-blank if Louis was alive! God knows what they're saying. Pretty soon, if they don't watch out, Rick Starrett is going to think he'd better come around and investigate a little more thoroughly.

Marietta invited them to the party the other day when she came in to see how the work was progressing on the booths for her restaurant. Marietta said the invitation was a thank-you for getting the booths done on extremely short notice and doing such a good job, considering all that had been happening, but Dixie knows Marietta invited them because, since the shooting, they've become local celebrities. Shane was his usual mean self, not saying anything he didn't have to, and Marietta was fascinated and a little frightened. "You'll come to the party, won't you, Shane?" she asked, and he scowled at her. "Bring Louis, if he feels up to it." She had the nerve to add that.

It's funny how something so bad, like the shooting, can have unexpected benefits, like the party invitation and the increase in business. Customers are still coming in with their sofas and chairs, from farther and farther away as the news spreads—three women came over from Breckenridge last week. They're almost always women. Dixie handles their orders and helps them pick out fabric while they sneak timid looks at Shane.

There's more work than they can handle. She's been telling Louis he'd better get his hand back in action so he can help out. She took him over to Doc last week and Doc was amazed at how well it had healed; he said Louis should be able to do anything he wanted to with that hand. It thrilled Dixie, when Doc took the bandages off and she saw Louis's raw, mangled hand, to think she was the cause of it. She longed to place that hand between her breasts to comfort it. But Louis isn't interested in trying anything with that hand except feeding his face and rolling his joints.

He's smoking one right now, lying on his bed, watching

Dixie go through his clothes. "We have to decide what you want to be," she tells him, "you know, a gambler, a gunfighter— I saw a neat gambler shirt—"

"No." He blows smoke toward the open window.

"Yeah. Gambler isn't right. You have to find the story inside of yourself first before you can know what your costume will be. Your story—"

"I don't have a story."

"Everyone has one. Even if you don't have one, that's your story. You see?"

He pulls on his smoke and holds his breath, looking at her until his eyes start to bug out.

Some of Louis's old shirts were really nice once. You can tell by the buttons. He must have brought them with him when he came from Rhode Island.

"Everyone who wasn't born here came because of a story. You know why I came? Because I wanted to live in a log cabin on a country road. I could just see it, you know? Like it was already waiting for me. Only, of course, it wasn't, and my story turned out to be a whole different thing."

She finds a shirt that isn't too bad, would look okay if she washed and ironed it. There's a Brooks Brothers label inside. "You're the stranger from the East who comes to the frontier to escape his past, which nobody knows about. Everyone thinks he's just a soft Easterner, you know? Then one day he does something really heroic that no one would have expected. He stands up to the gunfighter who has the whole town terrorized." Dixie picks up a pair of jeans. "I'm going to wash these too, in case I can't find anything better."

"What happens?" he calls after she's already through the door.

"What?"

"To the Easterner, with the gunfighter."

"He gets killed."

He looks so disappointed that she says, "Oh, maybe not killed, but wounded real bad. And he kills the gunfighter, and the gunfighter's girlfriend nurses the Easterner back to health. It turns out the Easterner always secretly loved the gunfighter's girlfriend. That's what gave him the courage to stand up to the gunfighter in the first place."

"I can't see getting into a fight over a woman." Louis holds the end of his joint with a tweezer so he can smoke the last bit.

"It was just a story." She leaves him there. The place stinks of marijuana.

Shane is walking around Marietta's booths, looking them over. The whole back of the shop is full of black-and-white cowhide benches, like cattle in a corral, and Shane in his Stetson and bandanna is riding herd. It's part of Shane's bargain with Louis that he's working in the shop until Louis can get back to it. Louis isn't doing Shane any favors by not pressing charges against Shane and calling it an accident, because Louis doesn't want the law snooping around and stumbling onto his marijuana room. So the two men are forced into a partnership, although neither one will speak to the other.

"How is he?" Shane points his chin to the ceiling.

"Mean. And stoned, but I saw him roll a joint with that hand, so he should be able to come back to work soon."

"It can't be soon enough for me. I didn't give up everything and move out West to make goddamn pleats on goddamn sofas."

"But you're real good, you know? The way you did the corners on the booths—it took me months to learn to do them that good."

Shane looks over his herd of booths with what might be mistaken for pride. "As soon as he's well enough, I'm getting out of here and you two can have the place to yourselves."

"I'm probably going to leave too. Louis isn't—he isn't interested in me anymore, and I can't say it's much fun working with you and living with him, when neither one of you will give me the time of day." She whips her hair around and stalks out. Shane goes back to stuffing some sofa pillows with kapok. He had been assuming, all this time, that Dixie and Louis were sleeping together up there, not that it bothered him, but now that he knows they aren't, he feels a little different. Louis is probably scared to touch Dixie because Shane is working downstairs.

Shane plunges his hand into a bag of kapok and remembers how sweet and silky Dixie can feel. He mounds it into the casing and remembers how her breasts fall when she's on her back. The ceiling creaks overhead—Louis, walking carefully, as if there were a wild beast sleeping below and he didn't want to rouse it. Shane grins and plumps the pillow. It's springy under his touch.

The Last Roundup was Buzzy's wedding present to Nadine so she would quit working at Eden Glen nights and weekends and have more time at home with him. Dixie stops in with the idea of finding some costumes for herself and her men, not to buy but rent, and not really rent but trade for some upholstery work.

"I love this—" Dixie fingers a deerskin jacket hanging from a post in the center of the store. It's creamy soft, nearly white, with turquoise beads on the yoke and back. "Louis would look beautiful in it, with his light hair—"

"Anyone would. But I can't lend that out, Dixie. It's part of the decoration. I don't expect anyone to buy it. It's just to draw them in, you know," Nadine says.

Dixie looks at the price tag. "One thousand one hundred thirty dollars. I guess you don't have to worry about anyone walking out with it on their back. No one I know, at least."

Nadine helps Dixie find a black hat and brocade vest for Shane, a black holster, and a toy six-shooter that looks real. A frock coat for Louis, no hat because his hair will look beautiful if he'll just let Dixie wash it, a shirt with a standup collar, and a string tie.

"You know, Dixie, you really are creative. I always think of Louis as a mousy character—he's always got threads hanging off him—but the way you're dressing him, he'll look like a poet. I can't wait to see him in this."

"Yeah. He is romantic. I mean, you know, he's mysterious if you think about it. He's kind of hiding out here."

"Where's he from?"

"That's the thing, you know, nobody knows where he's from, not even me, and I know him better than anybody. I think he comes from money and there's a secret in his past."

"He sounds like someone out of a Treat Redheart book."

"Yeah. The Easterner with a past."

Nadine pulls out a calico gown for Dixie. "Isn't this cute? You could wear the bonnet too." She puts the bonnet on herself, and it does look sweet on Nadine, but Dixie was thinking of something more in keeping with her new reputation as a woman men shoot each other over.

"You sure took your own sweet time. I thought you were making those clothes instead of washing them," Shane says.

She bounces in, arms full of bags, and throws everything on the sofa he's been slaving over all day. "That's the thanks I get? I was doing things for you."

"What kind of things?"

"I was persuading Nadine to lend us some clothes for the party."

"What party?"

"Marietta's. Remember, she said it was costumes."

"I'm not going to any fucking party."

"I explained it to you. I don't even want to go, but I'm doing it for you. To stop the rumors."

"What kind of costume?"

She pulls out a black hat, takes out a black-and-silver vest. Shane puts them on. He can see himself walking in wearing the vest and the hat.

"Look. She even had a six-shooter and holster."

"That's going to stop rumors? You really are nuts. I'll look like a gunfighter."

"Yeah, I know. It's like a joke, see? You wouldn't wear a six-shooter if you really did shoot Louis on purpose, would you?"

He straps it on. It fits. Shane used to wear a gun and holster all the time when he was a kid, a toy one of course. He draws.

"Oh! You're good at that. You look real."

"This isn't loaded, is it?"

"See? It even fooled you! It's a toy, but it looks real, doesn't it? It's a cap gun."

Shane doesn't know much about revolvers. He's never handled a real one. He twirls it and drops it in the holster. He smooths his hair and readjusts the hat, settles the belt on his hips. "I think I've got a white shirt that would go good with this vest."

"Now turn around real slow, like you feel someone coming up behind you," she says.

He looks at her over his shoulder, then wheels around and draws at the same time. She squeals. "Honest to God, you look right out of a movie!" She's shiny and cute like she was the first time she came into town, and she stands up close so he feels tall next to her.

When he takes her down on the sofa, the same one he stuffed this afternoon when he was thinking about her, his blood sings in his ears and races over all the stone walls in his brain, breaking them apart, dissolving the minerals, so that when it's over and his head is resting between her breasts, he can't remember what it was that kept him away from her for so long.

"What took you so long? I saw your car drive in an hour ago. What were you and Shane doing that made him stay late?" Louis asks.

"You washed your hair! Finally. It looks nice." Dixie runs her hand through it. "Shane was trying on his costume, that's all."

"You got him a costume?"

"I got one for you too, down at Nadine's store. Oh, you don't know about it of course, because you never go out or talk to anybody. It's called the Last Roundup and she has all kinds of things there. Just try this jacket. You see? It fits like it was made for you. 'Course, you don't have any mirrors up here, so you can't see yourself. Look at the window. Can you see yourself?" He looks into the window—black from the night outside—and even turns so he can look at his back. "Now take off the jacket and try it with the shirt underneath." She takes off the shirt he was wearing and helps him into the new one.

"Now you've got to start using that hand." He tries to pull it away, but she brings it to her lips and kisses all the red parts, the skinned parts. She takes the mangled web between his thumb and forefinger into her mouth and sucks on it gently. She places the hand between her breasts. "See if you can unbutton all these buttons." Dixie watches Louis's crippled hand making its slow, painful way down the front of her shirt and she knows that this is what she wants, all she wants.

CHAPTER 16

. . .

Waiting for Love at the Crossroads of the World

How many old-timers remember when that hippie kid camped at the corner of Main and Hoyt Streets? He had a crate to sit on and a tarp for when it rained. It seems he and his girlfriend had had a falling-out in Durango when they were hitchhiking across the country and had lost track of each other. So the kid decided that if he stayed in one place long enough, she was bound to pass by and they'd be reunited. It was an interesting theory, but the kid lacked the courage of his convictions. He disappeared after the first October snow. Residents with a scientific bent of mind still check out that corner now and again for signs of a hippie girlfriend passing through.

—from the Priest Creek *Crier*

DUSTY PICKED UP his mail at noon, but he goes by the Post Office again just before it closes and glances at the window of Lily's postal box. It's stuffed full of letters, notices, catalogues. Lily gets a lot of mail, from those organizations she belongs to and from fellow sheepbreeders, mule trainers, you name it. He still has the key to Lily's postal box. He was hoping she'd come by during the day when she could have one of the clerks open it for her, but she didn't. It's the second day she hasn't picked up the mail. He should leave it—if she doesn't care, he shouldn't either.

"I guess Lily and Foster are too busy up there to come down for their mail." Dixie giggles to see Dusty jump as if he'd been caught doing something illicit. He stuffs Lily's mail into his bag of groceries.

"I must say you're looking well," Dusty tells her, and means it. Everyone says that the situation over at Louis's is going to blow apart at any second, that walking into the shop is like entering a mine right before the dynamite goes off, and yet Dixie has never looked better. Which proves what Dusty's suspected all along, that Dixie thrives on disaster.

They meet Marietta on the way out. Dusty is her fair-haired boy ever since his piece "Bibleback Burton: Tragic Love Story of the Old West" appeared in *Western Life*. To capitalize on the story, she's named her big real-estate development up on Disappointment Pass "Burtons Ranch Preserve," and she's made certain there are copies of *Western Life* in every realtor's office. She takes Dusty's arm cozily and tells him to bring his guitar to her party so he can play some of those Western tunes he does so well. Dusty had been planning to go to the party with Lily, but he tells Marietta he doesn't think he'll be coming.

"But you have to! Tell him he has to," Marietta appeals to Dixie, whom up to now she hasn't seemed to notice. "And wear something Western. What's your usual fee? Five hundred?"

Dixie snorts. Everyone knows fifty dollars and free beer will buy you all the Dusty and his guitar you could stand.

"Five hundred should do it," he says.

"And of course I'll reimburse you if you buy or rent a costume."

"What's wrong with what I usually wear? Isn't it authentic enough?"

"I was thinking of something special—maybe dressing to look like the hero of a tragic love story of the Old West—"

Dixie puts her arm through Dusty's other arm, the one not already appropriated by Marietta. "I'll take him down to Nadine, Marietta. Nadine'll fix him up. You won't believe what she's done for me 'n' Shane 'n' Louis."

Marietta says she can't wait to see. Her party has all the earmarks of a legend in the making.

"Five hundred dollars plus expenses." Dixie, prim and wifely, steers Dusty into the Last Roundup. "Hey, Dusty, how about this, since Marietta's paying." Dixie holds up a fringed jacket.

"That would be great. If they ever ask me to sing in Las Vegas, it would be just the ticket," Dusty says.

"Guess how much it costs."

"I don't know, Dixie. How much does it cost?"

"One thousand one hundred thirty dollars."

"It's just decoration." Nadine rescues it from Dixie's hands. "I don't expect anyone to buy it."

"Hey, Dusty, 'Happy trails to you . . .' " Dixie sings, waving a white cowboy shirt with gold trim.

"I was thinking of something with more soul, less glitz," he says. Finally he finds just what he wants in a trunk Nadine hasn't unpacked yet.

"You oughta have that thing sprayed before you wear it," Dixie says.

While Lily has been getting lunch ready, Foster has been going through the notices and schedules that Lily has put up on the refrigerator door. He's pretending to help by throwing out the old ones, but she knows he's snooping.

He's like an animal that's been away and has to sniff out every corner to see what it has missed. "What's this?" He holds up the invitation to Marietta's party.

"It's one of those things where the whole town goes. You wouldn't like it."

"But you were planning to go. You kept the invitation. If I hadn't come—"

"I was thinking about it."

She would have gone with Dusty and all their friends. It's odd, but other times that Foster has visited, he's been lucky to get Lily alone because she has so many social plans, and this time, nobody has called or stopped by. Lily hasn't ventured off her own land, not even to pick up the mail. He feels that she's putting her life on hold until he leaves. Is she ashamed of him for some reason? "Let's go. I think it will be fun," he says.

She takes the invitation from him and drops it in the garbage. "No, it's too late. You're supposed to come in Western dress."

"So what? You have enough things here—"

"People are making a big deal out of it, getting really dressed. You know Nadine, don't you? She's been renting costumes out of her store for weeks."

"So we'll go in something substandard. I need to get out. I'm beginning to feel like your love slave; you've had me chained to the bed since I got here."

Lily laughs, but he's hit on a truth—she feels safe with Foster only when they are making love. This morning she begged him, almost ordered him, to stay in bed while she did the chores, but he insisted on dressing in Dusty's coverall and gathering the eggs. Coming back with them, he tripped and the basket went flying. It was no big deal, just broken eggs, but Lily didn't like seeing him that way, sitting in egg yolks and shells. She didn't like it when he went to help her nail the ram's head to the side of the barn and he turned pale and had to sit with his head down until he felt better.

Foster retrieves the invitation from the garbage and wipes off a corner where it came up against some coffee grounds. Last night, Lily's mother called three times. Lily explained it by saying that while Dusty was staying here he spoiled her mother by flirting with her, and now her mother keeps calling, hoping to get Dusty. Foster also learned that Dusty cooked Lily's Thanksgiving dinner and invited their friends. The man never made it to Lily's bed, but he infiltrated every other area of her life. And Foster's place has been narrowed to the confines of the bed. Foster checks his watch. "There's plenty of time to do some shopping at Nadine's. Let's go. It will do us good to get out."

Nadine is a little distant when Lily walks in with Foster. It's because Dusty was staying at Lily's so long; it gave people ideas. Lily tries not to let herself be bothered by what other people think, even if those people are friends. She does wish Dusty would call or stop by, however. He hasn't even come back for his things.

Foster goes immediately to a fringed jacket that Lily noticed before, hanging in the middle of the shop. "This is fantastic. Lily said all the good stuff would be gone by now."

"Oh, I can't rent that, Foster, it's—"

"Not rent. I want to buy it," he tells Nadine.

"Buy it?"

"It's amazing." He puts it on and turns so he can see the back in the mirror. "You like it, Lily?"

"It's a thousand—over a thousand dollars," Nadine says.

"You can take a check, can't you?"

"I guess."

"It's just a party, Foster. Look, here's a shirt for twenty-five."

"No, I really want this jacket. I'll wear it other times too. Look at the work on it."

"If you want it, I guess I have to sell it. This is a store after all." Nadine helps Foster take the jacket off. She folds it and wraps it in tissue paper. Foster brings out his checkbook, but he's still roaming the store. "How about you, Lily? Let me buy something for you too."

"I'll just rent something."

"No, I want to buy you a dress. I want you to look special."

Nadine helps Foster find a calico dress and bonnet for Lily. "She'll look like a little doll in this," Nadine tells Foster. Lily examines herself in the mirror. Could she look like a doll? But she lets them dress her and fuss over her because all she can think about is getting Foster back home.

Before they go, Nadine insists that Foster has to have a "real Stetson." He buys a high-crowned, wide-brimmed one with a snakeskin band. "You are going to look like such a dude," Nadine says, while Foster writes the check.

When they get home, they see that Dusty's left Lily's mail and the key to her postal box on the table. Lily looks for a note from him, but there isn't any.

"He must have cleaned out his stuff," Foster calls from the mudroom. "He took his work clothes and his boots. I wonder what he thought of that egg mess all over them." Foster hangs the coverall they bought for him today on the same hook where Dusty's hung. He steps back to admire it as if he'd just put up a trophy.

CHAPTER 17

Death of Bibleback Burton

The Old Hermit Who Has Long Been Known to the People of This City as Bibleback Burton Passed Away Last Sunday Evening

Last Sunday evening at a late hour the dead body of Bibleback Burton was brought down from his cabin on Disappointment Pass and taken to Lyden's undertaking establishment to be prepared for burial. For the past seventeen years the hermit has lived a life of almost utter seclusion in his little log domicile, his only companion and associate being a dog.

ELLIE HAS WRITTEN across the top of the Xerox, "From the *Crier*, 1902." She handed it to Dusty today when he went to return some books—something she'd found in the archives, she said. She can look like a cocker spaniel with her heavy, chin-length hair, her dark liquid eyes, a cocker spaniel who's been wronged by someone she respected and trusted.

Dusty pours himself a whiskey and smooths the copy out on the kitchen counter. What does it prove—only that Bibleback didn't end it all in Sulfur Cave. The rest could still be true. Four thousand copies of *Western Life*, with the lead story—"Bibleback Burton: Tragic Love Story of the Old West"—advertised on the cover, are lying in real-estate offices, doctors' waiting rooms, in the magazine sections of bookstores, in the Denver airport. He takes the whiskey out to the deck, stepping around the holes. Below, the creek mutters in the dark, feeling its way over stones, sighing its sulfurous, rot-reeking breath like some disgruntled ghost, the restless shade of a hermit long gone.

It's the damnedest thing, but Dusty can't remember what parts were true and what parts he made up. From what newspaper clipping, what bill of sale, did Dusty glean the information that Bibleback fell in love with his brother's wife? And yet Dusty believed it. He'd even convinced himself, finally, about Sulfur Cave. He was as shocked as Ellie to read the clipping.

He goes in to pour another finger of whiskey. He puts on his reading glasses.

... Henry Worth of the Western Union Telegraph Office and Shelton Stiss were last Sunday afternoon strolling through Elk Park up on Disappointment Pass. When they neared the dwelling the dog rushed out to them and, by pitiful whinings and almost human manifestations, induced them to go to the cabin. There they found the hermit on his rude bunk, with no fire, the door open, and almost unconscious ...

He drinks down the rest of the whiskey and cracks the ice in his teeth. His movements in the sheepskin coat are stiff. The Bible he wears underneath, strapped to his shoulders, makes his arms feel robotic. They reach for the hat and place it on his head. He finds Bibleback in the bathroom mirror, staring back at him with haunted eyes.

Lorraine nudges the hem of his coat. He pats her on the head. "Stay here. I won't be long." He's in the truck before he remembers that Marietta is paying him five hundred to perform, which is the only reason he is attending this party. He goes back for his guitar. On the way out he folds the Xerox and puts it in his pocket.

Foster tosses his head and looks back over his shoulder. The fringe on his jacket sways. He never made it as a folk singer—was still doing small clubs and colleges when he quit. Still, reviewers wrote of his stage presence, his magnetism before an audience. That was a long time ago. But he works out, keeps his weight down, has all his hair, none of it gray. The beadwork and fringe on the jacket make his shoulders look broad. He worries sometimes that he gave it up too soon, went for the money and abandoned the dream. Maybe he had something to give people, something more than the perfect voice for selling shampoo. The light flashes off the beads when he turns—

"You really like that jacket," Lily says.

How long has she been standing in the doorway watching him turn in front of the mirror? "Lily, you look right out of a Saturday-matinee Western." He lifts her off her feet and twirls her around, "Hee-haw!"—an act to cover his embarrassment, but she isn't fooled. And she doesn't look like any Hollywood frontier woman either. She looks real: wiry, tough, wind-chapped. "Dresses aren't your thing," he says, then realizes his mistake. "Pants, jeans. You look great in jeans. You have a terrific ass." He holds her there. Great little ass.

Lily looks at the two of them in the mirror, Foster with his shiny hair that falls into place—a highly skilled piece of work, Foster's haircut—his white and even teeth. That jacket! Beside him is the woman in the calico dress. She has lines between her brows from scowling at the sun and a pink scar down one side of her face. Suddenly that vague uneasiness she's been feeling, the disinclination to take Foster to the party, becomes a palpable fear. She senses, like an animal might, danger lurking there. But how to tell him when he's so determined to go? "We look like we stepped out of different stories," she says.

"Is it loaded, Shane?"

Shane was practicing his draw outside his trailer, things he used to do as a kid, like dropping to one knee or whirling around and drawing at the same time. He feels dumb, being caught at it, even if it is only by Frankie, who has the mental age of a nine-year-old. He must have seen the whole performance, sitting quietly on his step, invisible in the dark.

"Why don't you turn your outside light on?" Shane asks him.

"The bulb burned out. Anyway, I see fine in the dark," Frankie says.

"Yeah, because I leave my light on so you don't need yours. You're using my light."

"I'm just waiting for Mr. Petrillo to come pick me up. I'm working at his restaurant. That's where I work now." He comes forward into Shane's light. "You look real good, like the bad guy in a cowboy movie."

Shane draws his gun.

Frankie throws his hands in front of his face. "Don't shoot!"

"Relax. It's just a toy. I'm going to a party."

"Marietta's?"

"Yeah."

"I wish I was going. Is Dixie going too?"

"Yep."

"I heard you shot Louis 'cause of her."

"Who the hell—naw, that's not true, Frankie." Shane pulls out his tobacco and rolls himself a cigarette.

"I guess it was a mistake. I just heard—"

"It was a mistake, Frankie. I want you to tell anyone

who asks you that it was an accident. Louis is my friend and her friend. As a matter of fact, I'm going over there now to pick them up and take them to the party."

"You are?"

Shane cups his hand and lights up. "Yep."

"I don't think you should do that, Shane."

"What?"

"I don't think it's a good idea, the three of you going together."

"Why not?"

Frankie backs away.

"Why don't you think it's a good idea? You want to explain yourself?" Shane steps closer.

Headlights catch them. They freeze like animals on the road. It's Petrillo. Frankie gets in without saying goodbye. Shane sits on his cold step and smokes his cigarette. Seeing Frankie like that, in the headlights, reminded him of something, a fight he had with Dixie once.

"Jiminy Jaysus. I can't believe how handsome you are. Just turn around. People are going to be amazed at you. You realize no one's seen you since that night? You're a mystery to everyone. Even Shane. People's eyes are going to be popping out. Look at you!" Dixie says.

Louis studies his reflection in the mirror she bought for him. Oh, he is pretty too. She's done wonders. She's been feeding and caring for him better than she's ever cared for anyone, and it shows. He's using his hand more and is even talking about going back to work.

"I'm kicking you out because I'm going to put my costume on now and it's supposed to be a surprise," she tells him. She takes off her clothes and watches herself in the mirror as she puts on the stockings and fixes the garters. She tries on a fancy pair of red pants with lace trim that she's been saving—neither Shane nor Louis has seen them.

Then there's a corset she straps on tight so her breasts mound over the top. The petticoat goes on next—Dixie's mother used to wear petticoats like this—crinolines—when Dixie was a little girl. She can see her mother running to the door, her crinolines brushing the sides of the hall, while a horn honked outside in the night. Then the dress goes over that. And the hair all tousled, some up, some left down. Finally, little high-heeled ankle boots. She opens the door and reads her power in Louis's eyes.

Lily and Foster meet the Turrells, Nadine, and Buzzy in the plaza, where they're waiting to get on the gondola that will take them up to the party. Nadine must have warned them that Lily would be coming with Foster, as everyone seems to be taking it in stride and there's none of the awkwardness that Lily felt with Nadine earlier.

"This is so exciting!" Nadine says. She's watching everyone passing by dressed like characters out of the Old West, most of them wearing something from the Last Roundup. "We should do this every year, make it a town thing." Nadine is a picture, in a dress and petticoats and a bonnet. Buzzy has a string tie and a black hat—Doc Holliday, Nadine says. The Turrells are wearing homespun woolen ponchos. They look more like their sheep than ever. Lily smiles to think what Dusty would say. From the gondola, they look out on dark bare slopes with gleaming white trails where the snowmaking equipment has been working. Buzzy remarks on what a good job they're doing, getting the mountain ready for Christmas skiers, considering that there hasn't been any snow.

Cora Burtons is supposed to look like a log cabin—polished Winchesters mounted on the walls along with shaggy buffalo heads, some moose, some elk, antler chandeliers, an open hearth where two cowboy chefs are turning a side of beef on a spit. But two walls are uninterrupted wraparound window, so the whole thing looks like a log cabin blown up to gigantic size and then exploded. Standing at the center is the hostess, monumental in deerskin and beads. Foster says something about how he's never seen such expensive kitsch, but no one hears him. They're listening to Buzzy tell how the logs are thirty feet long and had to be shipped from Idaho. Chris Turrell says the cowhides are from Wyoming. Some had to be stenciled black and white to look like the others. The group decides to nab one of the cowhide booths before it gets too crowded to find a seat. Foster goes for drinks. He's heading back with his tray when someone calls his name.

Foster doesn't recognize him at first, then sees Rob Chipman, a former folkie like him who's now a record company executive in New York. It seems he and his wife, Astrid, are out looking over property and have put in a bid on a two-acre lot, part of an old sheep ranch. There will be hookups for fax machines, satellite dishes, and common pasturage for horses. The developer invited them here tonight so they could see some of the local color. Astrid says she's fallen in love with Priest Creek, not like Aspen and Vail, a real Western town with real people living in it. Foster says he'll deliver the drinks and come back to talk.

Lily is deep into a conversation with the Turrells. Foster tells her he's met people he knows; he'll be back. Rob introduces Foster to another couple, people from Los Angeles who are considering buying in the same development. "It's one of the last good land buys in Colorado, near skiing," Rob says. "And the town is full of characters, that's what I like. Look at that guy."

Rob motions to a large man in a mangy sheepskin coat and hat. Foster has the feeling he was looking at him and just turned away. "I know him. That's Dusty," Foster says.

"You know people here?"

"I'm staying with a woman who has a ranch just outside of town."

"Foster's amazing," Rob says to the others. "We think we've just discovered this place and he's already in with the locals. No kidding, Foster, you know these people?"

"Oh sure. That guy there in the string tie? That's Buzzy, the town coroner—"

"Buzzy?"

"Buzzy, Dusty, they all have names like that. Come on, I'll introduce you . . ."

"Looks like Foster has found some friends," Buzzy says. Foster is crossing the floor with two couples who are dressed Western but look as if they come from somewhere else. They look like Foster.

As Foster leads the way, he sees Lily and the others through Rob and Astrid's eyes—Lily with her gray hair hanging artlessly from a center part, her freakishly big forearms, her scar; the Turrells, Buzzy, Nadine. They do look like characters. Foster introduces everyone around the table. "These people might be your new neighbors," he says. "They're thinking of buying in—what was the name of that place?"

"Burtons Ranch Preserve," Rob says.

"Is that right?" Lily says.

Dusty finds Marietta involved in setting up a five-piece band on an improvised stage. "They're Texans. I booked them through an agent in New York," she tells him.

"What did you want me for, to play with the band or what?"

She looks at him blankly, then sees his guitar. "No, for the break, Dusty. You can play on the break. Phew, what are you wearing?" She steps back and looks at him. "Who are you supposed to be, Ben Gunn?"

He turns so she can see the hump. "Bibleback Burton."

"Oh no! Bibleback was much more romantic-looking."

"He was a humpback, Marietta, poor. His only companion and associate was a dog. How romantic could he have been?"

"His hump was small and sexy, you know, like Byron's foot. Fellows, those drums should be moved a tad to the right—"

"He was a recluse. From time to time his brother, Ethan, lent him financial assistance, although his wants were few."

"Will you take off that ridiculous coat?"

"You wanted me in costume."

"I've changed my mind. You're probably giving everyone fleas."

"I have an old newspaper clipping that says Bibleback died in his cabin in 1902. He didn't walk into the cave. I don't think he ever loved Cora or anyone. He was a solitary man, an eccentric—"

"Dusty, I really don't have time for a history lesson now. As far as I'm concerned, I paid for Bibleback Burton and he's mine. I'm having his cabin restored and made into a gatekeeper's cottage. Listen to some of the names of the roads I've thought up: Lost Love Canyon Drive, Heartbreak Trail . . ."

Let me know when you need me, Dusty tells Marietta, and retreats to the bar, where he can sip whiskey and watch the people grouping and regrouping. Lily comes in with Foster, who's wearing the jacket that cost more than a thousand dollars. Dusty heard they were coming but he was hoping they wouldn't, that Lily would back out at the last minute. He turns so she won't feel him looking at her.

There are people here whom Dusty has never seen before—couples mostly, of a certain age. They wear upscale watches and display bonded teeth when they laugh. Strangers to each other, and yet they recognize a common tie and knot together on one side of the room. Dusty assumes they're friends of Marietta's who have flown in for the occasion, but as he watches her move among them, shaking hands, venturing a pat on an arm, he sees that her relationship to them is formal, businesslike. And who might these business acquaintances be? Might they be prospective buyers who've come to look at land in Burtons Ranch Preserve? The interweaving of purposes and motives, the subtlety of the way Marietta's mind works, goes beyond what Dusty had suspected. Not only is Marietta staging a show for the locals, she is using them as a living display for her prospective investors. So what if Priest Creek doesn't have all those cute Victorian houses like Telluride, so what if Butch Cassidy didn't rob the bank. The town is steeped in the flavor of the Old West. Just look at these characters.

Dusty shoves his glass forward for more whiskey. The alcohol is working. He can watch Lily and Foster get up to dance and it's as if he were seeing them through the wrong end of a telescope.

There's a disturbance by the door. Dixie, dressed up like a dance-hall girl from a cheap Western, with Shane glowering on one arm and Louis on the other, has just entered. Marietta bustles over to them. They're part of the show too. No doubt Marietta has filled her prospective buyers in on the shooting. Shane's hand flicks his coat back. Does Dusty see a gun? A gun and holster? Would Shane be that stupid?

Marietta has persuaded Foster and Rob to sing with the band. Lily is going back to sit with the Turrells, when Dusty comes up and asks her to dance. Dusty's a good dancer, does a real Texas two-step, which surprises Lily. "Isn't it funny, Dusty? All these years that I've known you, I guess we never danced together."

He draws her closer.

"What's that smell?"

"It's my costume. Like it?"

"It's authentic, I guess. It's probably the way Bibleback really smelled."

"How'd you know I was Bibleback?"

"Who else would you be?" She thumps the Bible under his coat.

"People forget that part when they dress up like someone from the past, what that person must have smelled like."

Foster, on the stage with Rob and the band, looks taller and younger. His skin glows. And his jacket is perfect. It's as if he knew when he bought it that he would be performing. Dusty turns her so that she has her back to Foster. Now she sees Dixie, so tarted up that Lily didn't recognize her at first, dancing with Louis. Shane's scowling at them from the sidelines. Shane's hand moves his coat back.

"Is Shane carrying a gun?" Lily whispers to Dusty. "I thought I saw a gun under his jacket."

"There's a holster belt, looks like. He might have a gun, but I can't believe it's loaded. Shane is impulsive, you know, quick-tempered, but he's not stupid."

"Dixie and Louis make a nice couple," Lily says. "He's nice-looking. I never realized."

Dusty watches Dixie snuggling up to Louis, putting both arms around his neck. "She's out of control," he says.

"You don't think she'd try to provoke a fight, do you?"

"I can't say it would surprise me. Look at the way she got them to dress. She's practically written the script. Let me go talk to Shane. If he isn't drunk he can be fairly reasonable. Hit the floor if you hear shots."

Buzzy and Nadine are dancing, but the Turrells are sitting in the booth. Lily joins them.

"Foster's a good singer," Chris says.

"Too professional. I like Dusty's voice better. It's not as

smooth. Foster sounds like a commercial, you know what I mean?" Irene says.

Lily's watching Dusty talking to Shane, an arm around his shoulder.

"Look at Dusty's coat. That's what the old-timers used to wear, the ones who lived up in the mountains with the flock," Irene says.

"Came down for supplies maybe twice a year," Chris says.

"Like an Old Testament prophet," Irene says.

The prophet in his shaggy coat is trying to calm Shane down. Shane is all twitchy angles in his fancy vest, his black hat. He breaks away from Dusty and walks out on the dance floor. The crowd parts. Shane taps Louis on the shoulder. Louis stiffens, but he gives Dixie over to Shane, who takes Dixie around the waist and begins to dance. There's a collective murmur of relief, or maybe disappointment, when Louis walks away.

The set is ending. Foster, caught up in his own performance, seems to have missed Dixie's drama. He's shaking hands, smiling, acknowledging compliments. He even stops to sign an autograph. He's coming back to the booth with his friends Rob and Astrid, talking to Rob about maybe doing a one-night stand at the Bottom Line in New York, just for the fun of it. Between the two of them, they have enough friends who'd come. Why not? Lily squeezes in to make room for Astrid.

Dusty's voice comes over the sound system: "Marietta asked me to sing a few tunes, I'm not sure why. Maybe she's hoping to clear the place out early, save some on the food and drink."

Foster looks at Rob. "Local talent," he says.

"Maybe some of you could join in and help drown me out. There's Ellie, our librarian. She's always whispering, so maybe folks don't know she's a fine soprano. Come up

here, Ellie. Nadine, Buzzy—help me out. Dixie, Louis . . ."
Dusty gets a dozen friends up on stage with him. He invites
the audience to join in, but Rob and Foster keep talking
right through the singing.

When Dixie came in with Shane and Louis, and everyone
turned to look, she felt like the lion tamer at the circus
entering the ring. And when she was dancing with Louis,
and Shane cut in, and the two of them looked at each
other, she got the shivers right up her middle. But now
Dusty has her standing between Nadine and Ellie, and
Louis is on the other end with Buzzy, singing his part.
Some of Marietta's friends are standing right next to Shane,
ignoring him like he's part of the furniture, while he stares
into his beer like he's not too interested in what's going
on and he might be leaving soon. Who are these friends
of Marietta's anyway? Dixie's been seeing them around
town. Dixie thought the party was supposed to be for
people who helped out on the remodeling, and half the
guests turn out to be strangers. They're the kind of people
who fly in when the skiing's good and stay at the fanciest
condos on the mountain. They go around Priest Creek in
groups and see only each other.

Dusty's choosing all the usual old songs they sing at
parties together. The last one, as always, is "So Long, It's
Been Good to Know You."

Afterward Dusty comes over to thank Dixie for singing.

"Don't come near me in that stinky old coat. I never
should've let you get it."

"C'mon, I'll buy you a beer."

"Everyone knows drinks are free tonight, Dusty." But
she follows him to the bar.

"Sometimes you are the strangest person, Dusty. I mean,
look how handsome Foster looks. He made an effort. I'm

not saying you have to spend a thousand dollars on a jacket or anything, but any of those things I found for you would've been better than this old—" Dixie hitches herself up on the stool, allowing her skirt to fall so her legs are visible up to the garters. Dusty arranges the skirt to cover her legs.

"Dixie, you have to start taking responsibility for your actions."

"Like you, Dusty?"

"Well, maybe I'm not the best example, but at least people don't get shot—just tell me one thing, is that gun loaded?"

"What gun?"

Dusty gives her a look.

"Oh. No, I mean, it's a cap gun. It looks real, though, doesn't it?"

Shane should not have come to this party. He doesn't belong. These aren't his people—none of the wranglers from Eden Glen, no one from the road crew. Where did all these strangers come from anyway? Dixie and Dusty, sitting at the bar, look shabby next to them, don't belong. Even Lily looks out of place in this crowd. The strangers are the insiders and the people who live here have turned into outsiders. "Pretty soon we'll be the people who used to live here." The thought comes into his head just like that and makes him sad. Marietta's talking to a tall guy Shane doesn't like. He can't tell who he is from the back, but he knows he doesn't like him. Then the guy turns his head so Shane can see his profile. It's that guest from Eden Glen, the Texan—what was his name? Conway. Shane downs his beer, hitches up his gun belt, and goes over to Dixie.

"Let's get out of here."

Dixie turns herself more toward Dusty.

"C'mon." He takes her arm.

"Let go of her." Louis, pale, his jaw set, comes out of nowhere. Shane had forgotten about Louis.

"Look, it's a fight," Astrid says.

"Where? Oh damn." Lily scrambles to get past Astrid.

"Ouch!" Astrid cries, but Lily doesn't stop. She pushes her way through the gathering crowd to where Dixie stands with Shane and Louis.

Shane draws his gun. Someone grabs Lily from behind and takes her down. Together they roll with the fall. She is held close and enveloped in a pungent smell, so strong that it blocks out light and muffles shots and screams.

CHAPTER 18

■ ■ ■

Shoot-out at Cora Burtons

Festivities held to celebrate the opening of Cora Burtons, formerly Chez Marietta, were interrupted last Saturday night when Shane Daley drew a toy gun on Louis J. Wesley. No one was seriously injured. However, many were pretty near scared to death, and Cora Burtons suffered some damage as guests jumped on tables and wrenched vintage Winchesters off the walls. The rifles were not loaded.

Buzzy Halprin, town coroner, calmed Shane down and a discussion ensued about what to do with him. Some thought he should be turned over to Sheriff Rick Starrett, but it was pointed out that Priest Creek doesn't have a jail, and firing a toy pistol is too light an offense for sending someone all the way down to the jail in Silver City. Shane was released on his own recognizance.

—from the Priest Creek *Crier*

MARIETTA SAID she couldn't have planned it better if she'd tried. Even the gouges on the new tables and the scars on the log walls didn't faze her. She said it would add the patina of legend, or something like that. Her prospective buyers were thrilled. Dixie's *opéra bouffe* turned out to be one more entertainment in Marietta's Western village theme park.

And Shane was the clown. Dusty left the party with him—sort of took him into his custody—got him down the gondola, and steered him into the Coyote, where Shane rolled a cigarette and smoked it, drank down a beer, and never said a word. Dusty ordered a couple more and slid one over to Shane. Shane looked at Dusty. "Shane isn't my real name," he said.

Dusty nodded and drank his beer—didn't have the heart to tell him after all he'd been through that Dusty never for a moment had thought that Shane might be Shane's real name. Then Shane told Dusty his life story. Dusty either had heard it or imagined or assumed most of it before, but he let Shane talk, because you have to tell your story before you can know what comes next.

After a while Dusty said, "It's time to move on, get yourself a gig at some guest ranch somewhere—New Mexico or someplace. You can still be Shane—"

"I never got hired full-time at Eden Glen—you know that, Dusty. I was just a fill-in when they needed an extra hand. I couldn't even make the grade of full-time dude wrangler. I couldn't hack it with the guests." He rolled himself another smoke, and lit it the way he does, with his hand cupped against an imaginary wind. He inhaled, then looked at his cigarette. "I took up rolling my own when I changed my name. Hell, I took up smoking then too."

After a while Dusty went to the men's room, and when he came out Shane was gone. No one had seen him leave.

Shane didn't say goodbye to anyone. He cleared his things out of the trailer, leaving only movie posters curling on the walls. Dusty knows, because he went over there with Marietta, who owns the trailers and the land—something Dusty never knew. Marietta says she's thinking of clearing the trailers off that strip and putting up a tourist information center. She's going to see if Petrillo would have room for Frankie at his house. Shane had left without paying the rent.

"Walk on out, you manufacturer of horseballs, you machine for eating oats." Dusty kicks Two in the sides. One, riderless, is following close behind, because Two won't go anywhere without One and One won't be left without Two. No wonder Eden Glen sent them back.

There's supposed to be a big low-pressure system coming in, bringing two feet of snow at least. That's what they're saying. But this morning the sky was the same implacable blue. It's as if someone had put a bell jar over Priest Creek. The weather keeps going around it. Dusty decided to get out of town and escape the inevitable endless conversations. He's sick of hearing them like the dry chittering of insects everywhere he goes, from the filling station to the Post Office—helpless insect conversations. It's up to God, they say, as if God if He existed would care about how many runs they were able to open for Christmas.

Dusty's taking the trail up Outlaw Hill, the same one he took with Lily last summer. If he doesn't look back he can fool himself into thinking that she's following on One. She was dreamy that day, in love, wanting to talk about it. Instead, he distracted her by telling a story—his own, as it turned out.

"Git on up there, Two." He slaps her flank. She lays back her ears. One dances up alongside. It must be the cave that's spooking them. Dusty dismounts and wraps the lead rope around a scrawny pine. One can go untethered; she won't wander far from Two. He continues on foot.

Now he smells it too. The inside of his nose prickles. Molecules of sulfur trioxide are reacting with molecules of water to form hydrosulfuric acid. It's a satisfyingly simple chemical equation, at least Dusty remembers it that way, written on the blackboard in his high-school chemistry class. It can't be that simple in real life. Probably all kinds of chaotic side reactions occur—double loop-overs, whirling eddies of electrons. Nothing is simple anymore. The prickle in the nose is not unpleasant ten feet from the cave. Inside, the fumes would be strong enough to turn all the water in the lungs to acid—hungry acid burning like fire.

His lungs were buoyant and light when he threw himself on Lily to save her life. Pandemonium broke out all around while the two of them lay in his sheepskin bower. The gun, however, was a toy. He let her up, brushed her off. The last he saw of her she was next to Foster and his arm was around her.

Closer to the cave the fumes are denser. There's more stinging in the nose, a watering of eyes, a sulfurous taste under the tongue. Dusty cavalierly let Bibleback walk into Sulfur Cave because it was an easy way to end the story. Dusty failed to place himself in the twisted body and take the nearly impossible steps, to feel the self-loathing rage that could make a crusted hellhole look like a blessed release, a doorway, an escape hatch. An emergency exit.

Bibleback has walked out of the cave—the real Bibleback, the hermit who never presumed or dared to love anyone except his sole companion and associate, a dog. But the real Bibleback has no substance for Dusty—no height, no width, no volume. No smell. It is Dusty's Bibleback, lover of his brother's wife, who has left his presence in this place.

Dusty knows how Bibleback took a branch and switched his mule across the flanks until she galloped off toward home; how he stood here feeling the sun on his face; how he looked at this same Engelmann spruce—this very tree —and marveled at the bark, a mosaic of violet, ocher, gray, and brown; how the wind stirred the branches; the ground darkened at his feet and he looked up to see a cloud like the hand of God shutting out the light. Dusty pulls the sheepskin coat closer around him. Back in town they will be squinting at the sky and talking about snow. How the mind resists. How it clings to minutiae, small matters of bodily comfort. The condemned man carefully walks around a puddle on his way to face the firing squad.

The opening of the cave is not as narrow as he thought. There is enough room to allow a man of generous size to rush past the flimsy barricade. That's the way to do it—go in very fast as deep as possible, holding your breath, and then—

And then the body takes over, gasping. It craves oxygen; it breathes deeply, eagerly, but instead of life-giving air, it is taking in the death-dealing gas. It's like breathing a sword.

Foster is wearing the jacket and hat he bought at Nadine's. Lily suggested that he might feel conspicuous getting off the plane in New York, but Foster didn't want to trust his thousand-dollar jacket to baggage handlers and there's no way to pack a Stetson. You have to wear it. Besides, he likes the way he feels in these things—more like someone who lives here than a tourist passing through.

The day after the party he showed Rob and Astrid around Lily's ranch. Astrid shrieked when she saw the ram's head on the barn. "Lily shot it," Foster said. "You shot it?" Astrid asked. Lily nodded and walked away. She was gruff with them, on the edge of rudeness, but Foster liked it. It made it more special to be her friend. "Watch out when she says, 'Is that right?' " he told Rob and Astrid. "It means she's being patient with you."

Foster's gotten used to what Lily doesn't ask and what she doesn't say. They haven't talked about when he's coming back, if he'll return for Christmas. Any other woman would. But most women are needy; Lily is self-sufficient. She feels that when he comes back she'll see him, simple as that. This is what Foster tells himself on the silent trip to the airport. It's a companionable silence, he thinks, but when the truck pulls up beside the terminal, he can't come up with anything to say without sounding trivial or hollow. "Well," he says, and touches her arm. She surprises him with a kiss that knocks his hat off.

He gets out, retrieves his bag from the back of the truck. He turns to wave, but the truck is already rolling away, like a sigh, an exhalation. Gears engage and Lily is gone.

Lily pulls to the side of the road and turns off the ignition. Her eyes fix on the sky and the scorched peak of Sunrise Mountain, but she is seeing Bibleback Burton walking into Sulfur Cave—Bibleback looking like Dusty dressed for Marietta's party. His hand is at his throat and every breath tears into his windpipe. She sees her father's midnight-blue Lincoln flying over the embankment, shearing tops from trees and dragging them along. Had he calmly, in a moment of suspended thought, watched his hands turn the car off the road, just as she watched her hands lay the reins on the side of Cordelia's neck, causing her to turn toward the fallen fence?

Lily hears the plane and sees it circling to gain enough altitude to get over the Divide. Her love, wearing the thousand-dollar jacket he didn't know enough not to buy, is looking out the window, calmly watching Lily's world get smaller and farther away.

Ellie intercepts Lily at the door of the Post Office. "Could we talk, Lily? It will only take a minute. It's about Dusty."

This talk that will only take a minute cannot be accomplished at the Post Office, however. Ellie persuades her to go to the Sunrise Café. Over coffee, Ellie hands Lily a Xerox folded in three parts like a business letter. It is a copy of an article from the Priest Creek *Crier*, 1902, about the death of Bibleback Burton.

"I don't know what to do. I showed it to Dusty—" Ellie's eyes are full of sorrow.

But Lily is smiling. She breathes in the comforting smells of coffee, toast, bacon. What a warm, homey place the Sunrise is. Maybe she'll spend more time here this winter, hang out with Dusty in his "office." "I hated thinking about that poor humpback killing himself. I'm glad he lived on in his cabin. It's a beautiful spot—"

"But don't you see? It means Dusty made the story up," Ellie says.

"He can write a correction, can't he? Doesn't history get rewritten all the time when new facts come to light?"

"But my point is, he didn't even try. If I found this article, why didn't he?" She leans closer. Her cheeks are flushed. "There's something I heard at Marietta's party, that Dusty got ten thousand dollars from Marietta for writing that story."

"What does Marietta have to do with it?"

"She needed something to glamorize those lots she's trying to sell up at Disappointment Pass. She's trying to upgrade the whole town, give it some history. She wanted a love story, so Dusty took this poor old hermit and made up a love affair, a suicide, and God knows what else about him."

The day Lily and Dusty rode to Sulfur Cave, when he told her about Bibleback Burton, she asked him how he knew all those details. Of course he made it up; he was inventing as they rode along.

"I don't know what to do, Lily. Maybe I should write a letter to the magazine and enclose a copy of this article."

"Don't do that, Ellie. Even though Marietta paid Dusty, I'm sure he didn't intentionally tell lies. He just got carried away with his own imagination. I bet Dusty's working on a way to make this right. Let's give him a chance."

"I don't want to think it was intentional . . ."

When she leaves Ellie outside the café, Lily feels as if she's repaid Dusty for saving her life at Marietta's party, or trying to save her life, by placing his body between her and what he assumed was a loaded gun. Dusty's heroism astonished her. Foster was indignant, said Dusty could have hurt Lily, although Dusty broke the fall with his body and left her unharmed. Foster called Dusty a grandstanding buffoon. Lily asked Foster to stop talking about Dusty. She wanted to think about him in her own way. He's been so close to her for so long that she hasn't really seen him.

The dress Lily wore to Marietta's party is in a bag in the truck. Lily takes it out and decides to walk around to Nadine's store the long way past Dusty's cabin. His truck is parked outside. As Lily goes to the door, Lorraine starts barking inside and nearly knocks Lily over when she opens it. Dusty? Lily fears something's happened to him, but she looks around the neat cabin and is reassured by the order. Dusty's bed, in the sleeping loft, has been made. She always assumed Dusty slept on a single mattress, but his bed is as wide as her own.

He must be out back. She steps on the deck and almost goes through a broken floorboard. The dog rushes past and runs to the stables. One and Two are gone. Dusty must have taken someone out for a ride. The dog barks as if she wanted Lily to follow. Again, Lily has a moment of unease, as if the dog were trying to tell her something. But Lorraine is probably disturbed because Dusty didn't take her with him. Maybe the person Dusty is riding with asked that he leave the dog at home.

Lily wonders if it's a woman. Lily doesn't know anything about that part of Dusty's life. Dixie laughed when Lily said she thought of Dusty as leading a monkish life in his cabin by the creek. Now that Lily has seen the bed, she can easily imagine Dusty bringing a woman back here after a ride. He'd give her something hot to drink. Maybe they'd have a bath together. The bathtub is unusually large and looks custom-made. It and the bed belie the Spartan character of the rest of the cabin. Lily sits awhile in Dusty's big armchair. The fabric on the arms has worn to mere threads. The whole place is neat but worn, shabby even. It occurs to her that Dusty might be, for all his occupations, barely scraping by. The ten thousand from Marietta would have been a windfall for him. Lorraine is pacing the room, looking at Lily every once in a while, whining, barking. The problem is, she's spoiled. Dusty takes her everywhere with him. "C'mon," she tells her, "you can go to Nadine's with me."

Dusty stumbles back, spitting, gagging, his breath roaring, his heart kicking. A mountain jay screams from the spruce, jerking his whole body, protesting Dusty's pantomime, his dumb show. Dumb show.

One and Two whinny. Their feet thud against earth. One appears over the rise and comes trotting right down to nuzzle him on the neck. Tears fill Dusty's eyes, although he is aware that their affection is motivated by self-interest. Who else would keep them underworked and overfed? He rubs One between the eyes where she likes it, unties Two, and mounts up. As they head down the trail for home, it begins to snow.

"Nadine, is it all right if Lorraine comes in?"

"Oh hi, Lily. Sure. If she doesn't slobber. Are you going to slobber, Lorraine?" Nadine bends to rub the dog's head. "It's her second visit today. She came in with Dusty earlier."

"Then you've seen him and he's okay?" Lily asks.

"He seemed kind of down, actually. You know, quiet," Nadine says. "He was wearing that coat, bringing it back to return, but I told him to keep it or throw it out. Did you smell that thing? Oh, that's right, you must have. Wasn't it something, the way Dusty shielded you with his body?"

"There was so much confusion that I never got a chance to thank him."

"You know Dusty. He wouldn't want you to make a fuss. I tried to tell him this morning about how he was a hero and all, but he wouldn't let me. He's funny, isn't he? So big and friendly and all, but shy. It's sweet. He thinks the world of you, Lily."

Lily takes the dress out of the bag. "I wonder if I could return this. I'll never wear it again. Maybe you could take off the cost of what it would have been to rent it and send the rest to Foster."

"Oh sure. Most everyone rented anyway. The only thing is, I gave Foster a little off on the dress to make up for charging so much for the jacket. I feel bad about that. I never expected anyone to buy it."

"It's okay. He must have thought it was worth it. It did look good on him—"

"It looked great when he was up there singing. I almost forgot that part because of all that happened after. By the way, you haven't seen Dixie, have you? She borrowed a lot of stuff that she hasn't returned—not that I'm surprised. I'll probably end up going over there and getting it myself. Lorraine, do you want to stay in or go out?" Nadine opens the door for the dog, but Lorraine stands in the doorway barking. Again Lily wonders. The sky has darkened.

"Speak of the devil," Nadine says. Dixie's Toyota comes rattling down the road.

"I have to leave the engine running. It won't start unless you push it," Dixie calls as she pulls up. She begins hauling clothes out of the car. A red crinoline flies in the wind. Nadine rushes to help. She takes the clothes and lays them on the counter, fussing over them, examining them for tears and stains.

"Don't worry. I was real careful with them," Dixie says, and then to Lily, "Did Foster leave?"

"I just took him to the plane."

"He sure looked handsome in his thousand-dollar jacket. Is it true he's thinking of building a place over at Burtons Ranch?"

"No. Where'd you hear that?"

"Oh, I don't know. Maybe I made it up. I just figured since he was hanging out with that bunch."

"He's a lot more like them than us," Nadine says. She brushes off the hat Shane wore. "How's Shane doing, Dixie?"

"He's gone. I went over the next day and found these clothes in his trailer but nothing else. God, I hope that man didn't do something desperate."

"He wouldn't move his things out if he was going to kill himself," Nadine says.

"He loved me, Nadine. And he's a jealous man, a passionate—"

"You and I have different versions of what love is." Nadine shakes the crinoline as if she's expecting something nasty to fall out.

"That isn't love to you, trying to kill another man—"

Nadine gives the skirt another shake.

"Well, it's love to me." Dixie stalks toward the door, but instead of leaving she begins going around the store, picking things up and putting them down hard, like a child who's trying to break something accidentally.

"I think we'll hear from Shane again," Nadine says. "He probably got a job over near Aspen or Breckenridge, repairing skis. He was just embarrassed."

"Why should he be embarrassed?" Dixie asks.

"Pulling a gun that turns out to be a cap gun? It's kind of childish."

"Dusty's the one who should be embarrassed, for knocking Lily down."

"That was heroic. He laid down his life—"

"Yeah, except he knew it was a cap gun."

"Dixie, don't you ever open your mouth except to make trouble?" Nadine asks.

"It's true. I told him it was a toy. I told him right before."

"Why would he do it, then?"

"He was trying to impress Lily. Everyone knows he'll do anything to get her attention."

Lily wanders off to look through Nadine's vintage cowboy shirts, but she's thinking of the night after her accident, when Dusty slept in the bottom of her house, like ballast in a ship on a stormy sea. She thinks of the way Dusty looked when Doc stitched up her leg, and of how he didn't tell her Foster was coming but brought him to her anyway. She sees Dusty wearing the sheepskin coat and the pretend hump, mimicking his own creation.

After a while she is aware of Lorraine barking and wind coming in the door. Nadine and Dixie are standing looking at the snow tumbling out of the sky and turning Paradise Road into a sheet of white satin. Down the middle comes Dusty dressed as Bibleback, riding Two, with One trotting alongside. He stops in front and smiles at the three women standing there.

"Foster leave?" he asks Lily.

"He's gone."

"I was wondering if you'd care to ride One back to the stable for me. I don't want her to get excited and start loping. Might be bad for her system."

Without a word Lily twines her hands in One's mane and hoists herself on, bareback. Nadine and Dixie watch from the door as the horses and riders are gradually obscured by veil after veil of thickly falling snow.

"That's beautiful," Dixie says.

"Yes."

"It's just the way Treat Redheart would've done it."

CHAPTER 19

. . .

That's the Way It Went

Those of you who have been following the legend of Bibleback Burton, both in the *Crier* and in the winter issue of *Western Life*, will be puzzled to see on page 7 the reprint of Bibleback's obituary as it appeared in the September 25, 1902, issue of the *Crier*. Ms. Ellie Stern, who is in charge of the town archives as well as the Priest Creek Public Library, drew our attention to this bit of arcana after the winter *Western Life* was on the stands. It was an unfortunate oversight. After additional research and some speculation, we have come up with this version of the way it went.

Bibleback did indeed go up to Sulfur Cave that day. He slid off his mule and whipped her across the hindquarters until she clattered down the trail, her lamentations ringing off the rim rocks and causing angels to sit bolt upright in their heavenly beds.

See him now, with his odd sideways walk, edging nearer and nearer to the cave. He welcomes the sting of poisonous fumes in his nose and throat. Tears flood his eyes. He wants to burn them out clear through to his brain and turn his tormenting consciousness to witless ash.

But something happens. Does his mule come galloping back to knock him from the jaws of Hell? Or is it Ethan, or even Cora, who, having followed at a discreet distance, steps out of the shadows to persuade Bibleback to go on living? These are romantic speculations, but farfetched. More likely (although we'll never know for certain, because this simple man never kept a diary), Bibleback's own body took over at the crucial moment and countermanded instructions from his brain.

Choking, retching, he fell back from the mouth of the cave. He stumbed over to an Engelmann spruce (still standing to this day—you can go up there and see it), and leaning against its trunk, he gulped great breaths of piney air while a mountain jay screamed from a branch overhead. At length, the sheepherder recovered sufficiently to make his way down the trail. He found a warm welcome from his mule, who had stopped to munch on some succulent grass at the first stream crossing.

The two returned to Bibleback's humble cabin at Disappointment Pass, where Bibleback lived on another dozen years, asking little of anyone, alone except for his dog and possibly the mule. (There is no further record of this animal.) Ethan seems to have forgiven Bibleback and from time to time assisted him financially, although the hermit's needs were few. Perhaps Ethan couldn't find it in his heart to blame a cripple for making one desperate grasp at love.

—from the Priest Creek *Crier*

DUSTY IS STANDING on his back porch for the last time, having his morning coffee, watching fluff from the cottonwood trees pirouetting over the creek. Lorraine has come with him to spend his last bachelor night and, as if sensing the significance of the occasion, has made short work of her morning rounds and is standing beside him. One and Two have long since taken up residence in Lily's barn. Their stable has been scrubbed out so the new owner, an artist from New York, can use it as her summer studio.

Dusty runs a hand over his chin. On impulse last night he shaved the beard. He looked in the mirror above the sink where the lather and whiskers swirled, to greet the naked jowls of a middle-aged man with the beginnings of a double chin. Who was he? A groom. Lily's soon-to-be and till-death-us-do-part husband. He smiled to put his new reflection at ease, but it continued to regard him with a wary eye.

He was awake all night, tossing, staring out the skylights, occasionally cursing himself for having listened to Nadine, who insisted that he spend this last night away from Lily because the groom shouldn't see the bride on the day of the wedding. At one point he looked up to see a star—or maybe a planet—disturbingly large and bright, like the eye of God looking down upon him. He watched the eye progress from one skylight to the next. He tried to see it as a benevolent eye. After all, hadn't Dusty been granted his heart's desire? But increasingly the eye seemed to threaten and warn. Too much happiness coming to a man who'd learned to live with less. Too much to lose. And its relentless procession reminded Dusty of time's passage and how he and Lily have already reached the middle of their lives, and how quickly the rest will slide away.

Change, beginnings, even good ones, unsettle him. He has to remind himself (as he looks over the creek with the cottonwood seeds courageously riding downstream to their own beginnings or ends) that the river is always flowing, you never step in the same water twice, and standing still is an illusion. That's when minerals creep in and turn bone to stone. "Sail on down the river of time!" cries the middle-aged groom. The dog looks up at him and barks.

"Oh, Lily, you look beautiful with all this puffy stuff floating around you. You are going to love this picture," Nadine says. She came over to help Lily get ready. The wedding dress is Nadine's gift, an antique she found at an auction outside Durango. She's brought Lily out on the deck so she can take her picture.

"Back home we used to call them wishes," says Dixie. She reaches out from her perch on the fence and catches one of the seeds floating by. She holds it on her fingertip and closes her eyes. She used to do this a lot. Hot urgent wishes would come out of her, wishes too heavy for the fragile puffs to carry off to—where were those wishes supposed to go? To your guardian angel up above? Dixie blows on her finger. The fluff spirals up unencumbered.

"What did you wish for?" Lily asks.

"Nothing. I don't make wishes anymore. I make plans."

"Dixie, mind what you do in that dress. You could tear it on a nail or something," Nadine says. She has outfitted Dixie in a flower-sprigged gown similar to the one she is wearing. They will be Lily's attendants. Buzzy is going to be best man.

When Dusty and Lily decided to get married, they were thinking of a small ceremony, but as they began telling their friends, they realized everyone was counting on a big wedding, so Dusty and Lily turned it into a community event. The whole town is invited to the ceremony at the top of lift 10, to be followed by a potluck supper. Marietta is contributing the lift free of charge, as well as something she's calling an ox to be roasted over a spit.

Dusty told Lily's mother over the phone. She was so excited that she said she was going to come to the wedding, and Dusty, being Dusty, said great and asked her to save him a dance. Lily had to remind Dusty of the way it is with her mother—the alcohol, the pills, someone in attendance at all times. How could they have her at the wedding? How could they refuse if she wanted to come, Dusty argued. They were both relieved when she called a couple of days ago and canceled because her hair wasn't coming out right.

"Hey, Lily, you'll never guess who I saw yesterday walking down Main Street big as life and twice as handsome," Dixie calls out.

"The bridesmaid is supposed to calm the bride, not make her even more skittish than she already is," Nadine scolds.

"Who?" Lily asks, but she already knows.

"Foster, wearing that fancy beaded jacket. He's staying with Astrid and Rob. I bet he'll be at the wedding too, but he didn't say."

"He wouldn't dare," Nadine says. She puts the camera down as if she's seen something in Lily's face that shouldn't be documented.

Lily thinks Foster just might come. The Turrells have taken Cordelia and Simone up and will have them ready for after the ceremony, when Lily and Dusty ride off for a couple of days' camping along the Divide. She pictures Foster on Cordelia, Simone's lead rope in his hand, galloping up to Lily as she waits at the altar. He leans down like a trick rider and scoops Lily up. The two of them ride off, her torn veil flying in the wind.

"Lily, now what's so funny? I can't take a picture of you like that," Nadine says.

"Nadine, you are such a fusspot today. You'd think it was your own wedding instead of Lily's. Why don't you set the camera on remote or something so it can take a picture of the three of us."

While Nadine sets up the camera, Dixie comes over and puts her arm around Lily's waist. "This is going to be some beautiful wedding. I think me 'n' Louis will get married up there too—in winter on skis. Louis took up skiing last winter and he was pretty good at it."

"You and Louis are getting married?" Nadine asks.

"He doesn't know it yet, but we're definitely getting

married." Dixie only got the idea just now, standing next to Lily dressed like a bride, with wishes floating all around. But Louis will agree. Since Marietta's party when, in Louis's mind, he stood up to Shane and won Dixie from him, Louis has become a changed man. He considers himself a town hero, even if nobody else does. He's become real friendly with the customers, and even started going out to town events with Dixie. Being a married man will go well with the new image Louis has of himself, as a man of the community instead of some lost boy hiding out in a cloud of marijuana smoke. Before they marry, Dixie will insist that he buy her a cabin on a country road. Looking back, Dixie finds it hard to believe how much she's accomplished in less than a year, after a lifetime of false starts. Now she's going to have everything she ever desired: the cabin with the ponderosa in the yard and a goat tied up under it, maybe even a baby—why not?—and on the porch her sad-eyed man.

Foster did not come to Priest Creek to attend the wedding. He merely stopped on his way to Los Angeles, where he is scheduled to tape a commercial next week. He came to see Astrid and Rob, who are renting a place in town while their house is being built in the Burtons Ranch Preserve. Meg had informed Foster about the wedding plans but hadn't mentioned the date. Or maybe she had but he had forgotten. There was some awkwardness when Rob and Astrid realized that Foster was going to be with them on the day of the wedding, because the whole town had been invited and Rob and Astrid had been looking forward to going. First they decided they wouldn't go after all. Then Astrid said maybe she'd go alone, as she hated to miss a community event. Astrid is hoping to run for County Commissioner, so it's important for her to get out and meet as many folks as possible. Rob and Astrid are committed to keeping Priest Creek from turning into "another Aspen."

Of course they should both go, Foster said. Then, at an auction in Silver City, he found the perfect wedding present for Lily, a gelding—pretty little thing with four white stockings. Astrid had told him that Lily and Dusty were starting up a business taking people out on pack trips. The gelding will be just what they could use. Foster's having it delivered while Lily's away on her honeymoon.

Foster is waiting his turn at the lift with Astrid and Rob and the other wedding guests. He's pleased with himself for finding a gift and attending the wedding in a magnanimous spirit. He went through some painful changes to get to this point. He was stunned when Lily dropped the news that Dusty was moving in with her. She just handed it to him over the phone. Foster didn't get it at first. "What do you mean, to help you out with the work—" Foster said. "No, as a—we're going to try living together as a serious thing," she answered. There was a long silence. Foster's usually good at phone conversations, but this time he was stymied. He was sure that if he were there beside her he could do something—touch her, anything. A small gesture would tip the balance, but what good were words over the phone? It was Lily finally who came through with the words. "It would have been different if you'd lived here. It's the times you go away, the times you don't call. I try not to let it bother me, but it does. I can't help the way I am." "But you never said, you never told me," he said. "Would it have made a difference?" she asked. He couldn't answer. What drew him to her in the first place was her independence and how little she seemed to need. Now she was telling him that she had to have everything. Could Foster give up his home, his work, friends, just to keep her?

Right after his conversation with Lily, Foster went to Bella, wanting to see his own disappointment mirrored, even magnified in her features, expecting her to tell him to hop a plane and fly out there right away. Bella made the appropriate maternal noises—too bad, she would have liked to meet Lily, a shame, but maybe it was for the best, difficult to work out a move to Colorado with Nicholas and all. Then she dropped her bombshell: she was getting married. To someone called Maynard, a psychiatrist. She told Foster she never dreamed another person could bring her such joy. She showed him a snapshot of a chubby, smiling, bald guy. Maynard.

Feeling dazed, a little lost, Foster left Bella's and found himself walking over to his old apartment, where his ex-wife and Nicholas still lived. His wife was on her way out, wearing a dress Foster had never seen before. "She has a date with Willy," Nicholas told him, as if Foster must know who Willy was. Not long after that, Willy moved in.

Spring came and Foster began dating a woman named Olivia. It lasted until summer. Then Olivia began using words like co-dependency. She's at a yoga retreat right now, learning to live without stimulants and solaces such as coffee, alcohol, sugar, and Foster.

The experience left Foster yearning for something he'd found with Lily and no one else. It wasn't merely his affection for Rob and Astrid that brought him here, and he's enough the child of psychiatrists to suspect that it might not have been a coincidence that he arrived just before the wedding.

There was something different about Lily—her four-horned sheep, the savage retribution she took out on the turkey—something closer to nature, closer to what a human should be. The night the sheep opened to reveal the lamb and Lily took Foster into her bed, Foster was transported to an ancient time when civilization was young and could be shrugged off like a coat when it got too heavy.

Foster came back this last time with a nebulous hope—

that he would see Lily in the street, or he would go to her house when Dusty wasn't there and it would begin again. Instead, Foster saw the two of them. They weren't doing anything special. She was filling the truck with gas while Dusty was coming out of the liquor store with a case of wine, for the wedding, no doubt. He saw how right they were together. If there were a game with the photographs of a hundred men and women lined up and he had to match them into couples, theirs would be the first photos he would choose—the identically weathered faces, the styleless but practical clothes. There was also something a photograph couldn't convey, a complicity, an unconscious body language, a way of communicating without speaking, the closed-circuitry of coupleness.

Lily and Dusty. They're living a dream. It was a dream that Foster succumbed to for a while—that there could be, in the late twentieth century, a small place high in the mountains above the smog line, a post-industrial paradise whose wealth lay in snow and sun, flashing streams and thermal springs, where a person could leave behind all the destruction that man has wrought and begin again, restored at last to a harmony with nature, this time with indoor plumbing.

Foster lacked the faith finally to buy into the dream. Maybe his view of life was too complex; you have to forget a lot to achieve a simple vision. He could manage it only for a week or two and then he would go back to what he considered real life. When he saw Lily at the filling station with her mate beside her, he wondered if his connection with Lily had ever existed, or if it was something Foster invented in the temporary weightlessness of switching from one culture to another.

"Are you coming, Foster?" Astrid, pretty in her fringed skirt, her boots, calls as she and Rob board a chair to the top.

"Single?" a young woman asks.

"Yes," he says, surprised by her audacity, but then understands that she is referring to, not his marital status, but the way he intends to ride the lift. She and a kid with blond dreadlocks slow it down and Foster jumps on, joining the parade of wedding guests in their make-believe clothes, floating over treetops, over canyons and crags, their feet dangling free. Feasting on air.

Dusty sees an unmistakable one-of-a-kind beaded jacket riding the chair lift and the small hairs on the back of his neck stiffen. Dusty had heard he was in town, although he didn't tell Lily, didn't figure the guy would have the balls to come to the wedding. Has he come to take Lily away? Will it be Foster, not Dusty, who rides off with the bride? Dusty removes the white Stetson Nadine insisted he wear for the ceremony and wipes his brow on a clean white nuptial handkerchief. He looks around for Lily. Nadine says it's bad luck to see the bride before the ceremony, but if he could just catch a glimpse of her he'd feel better.

A week or so ago, before he'd heard Foster was in town, Dusty had told Lily that they should have invited Foster to the wedding. "Why's that?" she'd asked, her wet head leaning against his chest. They were in the hot tub. "Because if it hadn't been for him, we might never have gotten together like this. It's like—think of life as a cliff—" She laughed. "And we were stuck on a ledge that wasn't very comfortable but seemed safe at least. And then Foster came and forced us to move onto a higher ledge," he said. She thought about it for a while, then said, "Are you going to invite him?" He leaned over and kissed her on the place where her hair parted. "No," he said.

He jumps on the lift, alone, but not really, because there's a whole train of people ahead of him who have come to wish him and his bride well. Maybe even Foster—he sees the jacket disappearing over the first ridge—maybe even Foster wishes them well. Dusty turns around and sees Buzzy and Nadine in the chair behind him.

"Dusty, you're not supposed to look!" Nadine scolds, but it's too late. In the next chair back are Dusty's silver-haired bride with her maid, the Queen of Chaos. In the air around them, like the souls of unborn children, cotton-wood puffs are dancing. Dusty waves. For a moment they don't know who he is without the beard. Then they wave their arms over their heads, crossing and uncrossing.